FROM IVAN REITMAN, THE DIRECTOR OF "GHOSTBUSTERS," "TWINS" AND "DAVE"

ARNOLD SCHWARZENEGGER DANNY DeVITO EMMA THOMPSON

Nothing is inconceivable.

AN IVAN REITMAN FILM

JUNIOR

UNIVERSAL PICTURES PRESENTS A NORTHERN LIGHTS PRODUCTION
ARNOLD SCHWARZENEGGER DANNY DeVITO EMMA THOMPSON
"JUNIOR"

FRANK LANGELLA PAMELA REED
MUSIC COMPOSED BY JAMES NEWTON HOWARD COSTUME DESIGNER ALBERT WOLSKY
CO-PRODUCERS NEAL NORDLINGER GORDON WEBB
EDITED BY SHELDON KAHN A.C.E. WENDY GREENE BRICMONT A.C.E.
PRODUCTION DESIGNER STEPHEN LINEWEAVER DIRECTOR OF PHOTOGRAPHY ADAM GREENBERG A.S.C.
EXECUTIVE PRODUCERS JOE MEDJUCK DANIEL GOLDBERG AND BEVERLY CAMHE
WRITTEN BY KEVIN WADE AND CHRIS CONRAD
PRODUCED AND DIRECTED BY IVAN REITMAN

Northern Lights
ENTERTAINMENT
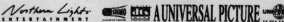
A UNIVERSAL PICTURE

JUNIOR

A novel by Leonore Fleischer
Based on a motion picture written by
Kevin Wade and Chris Conrad

JOVE BOOKS, NEW YORK

JUNIOR

A Jove Book / published by arrangement
with MCA Publishing Rights

PRINTING HISTORY
Jove edition / December 1994

ISBN: 0-515-11626-2

A JOVE BOOK®
Jove Books are published by The Berkley Publishing Group,
200 Madison Avenue, New York, New York 10016.
JOVE and the "J" design are trademarks belonging to
Jove Publications, Inc.

PRINTED IN THE UNITED STATES OF AMERICA

10 9 8 7 6 5 4 3 2 1

JUNIOR

Chapter One

Alex

The instinct to reproduce is one of the three basic human instincts, ranking only after the instinct to survive and the pressing urge to find a decent fat-free ice cream. Fortunately for the survival of the human race, the instinct to have children is felt in a vacuum—without any foreshadowings of the cost of nursery school, orthodontia, new sneakers, or six years of community college. A man and a woman who desire to be parents focus only on their blissful, roseate image of a cooing infant trying to fit its little toes into its cupid-bow mouth. If they could flash forward fifteen years, to that same baby as an adolescent—sullen, contemptuous, self-absorbed, smelly—the chances of their going for parenthood would be sharply—very, very sharply—reduced. The human race would soon die out, and cockroaches would take over the planet.

Wasn't it Euripides's barbarian princess Medea who declared, "I would rather stand in the ranks of battle three times than bear a single child?" Okay, bad example. Medea may not be your poster girl for Mother's Day, given that she chopped up her own children to get back at her husband when he left her for a younger princess, but what she was really saying still stands today, twenty-five hundred years after Euripides.

Men have it easy. Going to war (especially in Medea's day, when most of the battle consisted of men in helmets banging their spears on their shields and yelling across to the enemy that his mother was a goat) simply can't be compared to the blessed miracle of childbirth, which is like trying to push a checker cab through an opening smaller than a Frisbee. What Medea was trying to say was that men, who whine about having to shave, who rush to emergency rooms with a paper cut, have no idea how lucky they are to be spared what they are spared: menstruation, PMS, bloat, sore nipples, nausea, pregnancy and—you better believe—the excruciating pangs of childbirth.

Actually, in a number of primitive societies, there is a cute custom known as couvade, in which, when a wife goes into labor, her husband, in a fit of autosuggestion, doubles over and takes to his bed moaning and groaning and sweating and cursing, carrying on as though he's the one giving birth. Naturally, he hogs all the sympathy and attention. The dictionary connects the word "couvade" with the word "coward." 'Nuff said.

But we digress: consider the unique case of Dr. Alexander Hesse, a man for the nineties. Alex, fortyish, single, six feet four inches high and less than one percent body fat. Alex has it all: pecs, abs, delts, epsilons, biceps, tricycles, androids, and not an inch of pinch anywhere on him; you could scrub your overalls on his stomach. From his shoulders to his sneakered feet, everything about him is larger than life; on the rare occasion when Alex smiles, he doesn't smile so much as grin. Alex doesn't make small talk, he lectures, and he doesn't walk unless he strides. And the biggest thing about him is not his hands or his shoulders or his biceps—it's his brain.

Dr. Alexander Hesse is a gifted research scientist in genetic engineering at the famous Lufkin Center of the Biotechnology Research Center at Leland University in San Francisco, working on the development of a top-secret bioengineered formula called Expectane, and the work is going like gangbusters. Alex is now on the verge of becoming very famous and very rich, although to him, the success of his work and the benefits it will confer upon humankind are far more important than any amount of money or celebrity. Dr. Alexander Hesse is a very literal-minded person. He could not possibly have imagined the altogether bizarre adventure that awaited only the step of his size fourteen Nike.

We don't want to spoil any of the many surprises and shocks that await our hero. But before he crosses over that verge into that great unknown, before he sets forth on that adventure that will change the course of scientific history, let us just say that, in the words of the first-generation, politically-incorrect *Star Trek*, Alex Hesse is about to boldly go where no *man* has gone before.

Alex hit a few more keys on his computer keyboard, and the graphic on the screen began to revolve slowly, to show, first in profile and then in full-face, the body of a female ape, very pregnant. Around the picture were windows of calibrations and calculations, plus a revolving graphic molecular model of the compound Expectane, and the entire screenful of graphics was projected onto a large overhead monitor, where Dr. Hesse's graduate students could see it clearly and, presumably, understand it.

"The miscarriage-prone female reproductive system is merely an extension of the body's natural and necessary instinct to reject foreign matter. And from that equation comes the idea for Expectane," Alex explained without emotion.

The grad students bent dutifully over their notebooks and scribbled down Dr. Hesse's words verbatim.

Alex stood up abruptly and walked over to a large, comfortable cage containing two adult chimpanzees, Minnie and Moe. Minnie was obviously in an advanced state of pregnancy, the living model for Alex's computer profile, and Moe was the expectant father.

Alex put a couple of fingers through the cage bars and scratched Minnie on the top of her hairy head. He preferred the chimpanzee to most humans he knew. "Minnie here had a history of miscarriages. But as a result of our treatment, she is now in her seventh month of pregnancy."

Alex handed the ape a glass vial of a liquid substance, and she drank it down eagerly. "She takes twenty-two cc's of Expectane three times a day." Alex turned to scan his students, and his eyes went directly to the back of the lab.

"Bradford!" he called sternly. "There is no yawning in this laboratory."

Wanna bet? thought Bradford, but he wisely kept silent. Dr. Hesse wasn't noted for a sense of humor.

In sharp contrast to Dr. Alexander Hesse is Dr. Lawrence Arbogast, M.D., gynecologist co-owner of The Fertility Center. He has a well-developed sense of humor, and joking around is about the only exercise he takes. Larry is a foot shorter than Alex; when they walk side by side, it's as though they don't belong to the same species. Alex has a head of thick reddish-brown hair; Larry kissed most of his follicles good-bye years ago. Alex is

4

inner-directed, solitary, quiet, stern, and even sometimes intimidating in demeanor; Larry is outer-directed, affable, bossy, voluble, gregarious, engaging. As we said, Alex has a soul above money; money is the central fact of Larry's existence. Money is the pivot on which Larry's world merrily turns.

This odd couple are united by one thing—their partnership in Expectane, a drug which is designed to prevent miscarriage in precarious pregnancies. Alex has developed Expectane, and Larry has sunk a sizable chunk of his personal change into that formula, about $300,000 worth. It was an investment made less for its beneficial aspects than for the real opportunity of selling the drug to a giant pharmaceutical conglomerate for very big bucks indeed.

Where Alex Hesse is methodical, single-minded, and scientific in his approach to everything, Larry Arbogast is a tumbler and a juggler, keeping several balls twirling in the air at one time while, as a one-man band, he plays the cymbals with his knees. Alex works in a high-tech laboratory, all right angles and shiny, scrubbed surfaces. Larry's offices are in a beautifully renovated old San Francisco mansion converted into a state-of-the-art fertility center, with expensive draperies and bright brass bowls of colorful flowers, soothing art on the walls, and welcoming smiles on the faces of receptionists, nurses, and attendants. "Here," the fertility center seemed to be saying, "here baby makes three."

His collar open, his necktie in the pocket of his twenty-four-hundred-dollar suit, Dr. Lawrence Arbogast waltzed into The Fertility Center, chowing down on the last bites of his Egg McMuffin, throwing greetings right and left like a king chucking gold coins from his carriage to the peasants.

"Morning, Betty, nice hair. Yvonne, good to see you back. Hey, Ned!"

This last greeting was addressed to his partner in the Center, Dr. Edwin "Ned" Sneller, M.D., who fell in step with him, walking along the corridor to Larry's office. On the other side of Larry, flanking him, was his assistant, Louise Frascati, a dark-haired young woman with strong Italian features.

"Are you nervous about the hearing?" asked Ned.

Larry wiped McMuffin crumbs off his chin, slipped the tie from his pocket, and threw it around his neck, fumbling with the knot. "The FDA? Nah, it's a lock," he said confidently.

"When you get a chance, we need to go over our pension plan," said Ned, and he peeled off, heading for his own office.

Louise took over efficiently, running down Larry's appointments. "Mrs. Parrish is in Number One for a second-trimester sonogram. You've got an initial consultation with the Lanzarottas . . ."

They had reached the door of one of the examining rooms. An enormously pregnant woman was lying on her back on the examining table, her belly mounded like an Alp.

"And Mrs. Logan is here for her final," concluded Louise.

"Doctor, I'm ready to explode!" complained Mrs. Logan.

Larry smiled reassuringly as he pulled on a pair of fresh latex gloves. "Nah, don't worry. I won't let that happen. You'd mess up the wallpaper."

• • •

Alone in his lab, free of his students at last, Alex turned his full attention to Minnie, his star experiment. The chimpanzee was lying on her back on a lab table, bearing an uncanny resemblance to the explosive Mrs. Logan. Alex gently massaged her swollen belly, while Moe, her mate, the soon-to-be father, sat quietly at her feet.

"Absolutely perfect." Alex smiled one of his rare grins. "Just another month. Good."

"Dr. Hesse? It's showtime," called a chilly voice from the lab doorway. The autocratic voice belonged to tall, dark, and autocratic Noah Banes, the administrative head of the university's science department, a coldly ambitious career academic with visions of glory. Sooner or later, one of the department's research wonks would stumble across something Nobel-worthy, and then Leland's University's science department—and Banes, its administrative head—would come in for a share of the fame. Today, the university was backing Dr. Alexander Hesse's work in Expectane. Tomorrow . . . who knows? One of Banes's well-manicured hands came up and made minute adjustments to a perfectly tied bow tie and patted down the lapel of a J. Press tweed jacket. He was ready for a public appearance.

Alex glanced at the clock. Banes was right; it was already 2:30, and the FDA hearing was scheduled for 3:15. This was a crucial meeting with the federal Food and Drug Administration. Animal testing of Expectane was just about completed. The next logical step was to begin testing on humans—on expectant, miscarriage-prone mothers—and for this they would have to obtain FDA approval.

Alex tucked a thick folder of notes and lab results into his briefcase and clicked the locks. Alice, his lab assistant, quiet, dour, and efficient, handed him his jacket. "Good luck with the FDA," she said.

"Luck is for the ill-prepared," replied Alex soberly.

"Yes. If you need anything—"

"Yes." Alex finished her sentence silently. They had worked together so long that they understood each other without words.

On the other side of the city, in his elegantly appointed office, Dr. Arbogast was interviewing new clients—in the nonthreatening terminology of The Fertility Center, a patient was not a patient but a client—a couple in their mid-thirties who were having trouble conceiving a child. "One last question, Mr. and Mrs. Lanzarotta," said Larry as he had just about finished taking down their case history. "Any family history of infertility?"

"My brother shoots blanks," Mr. Lanzarotta said uncomfortably.

Larry put up his pudgy little hands in a show of protest. "Hey, we don't use those negative terms around her. I want to hear: 'I'm loaded for bear, and my aim is true.' Say it."

"'I'm loaded for bear, and my aim is true,'" Mr. Lanzarotta repeated, rather sheepishly. He looked at his wife, and both of them laughed, easing the tension a little.

"That's the spirit!" Larry grinned encouragingly. "We'll get started on Friday." The couple nodded agreement; already the Lanzarottas were feeling more positive about things; Larry Arbogast frequently had that effect on people. The doctor ushered them to the door, taking off his white coat and grabbing his suit jacket off the hook at the same <u>time</u>. He glanced at his watch. It was getting dangerously close to three; he had to be at the FDA hearing by 3:15 at the latest. This was D-Day, the day the FDA Investigational New Drug Review Board would make its decision for or against the human testing of Expectane.

He hustled down the gleaming corridor to the front door, taking nervous peeks at his watch. At his side, his assistant, Louise, scampered, handing him his briefcase.

"The car's waiting out front. I told him to check the traffic reports—"

"And the big dweeb?" interrupted Larry, referring of course to his partner, the well-respected research scientist Dr. Alexander Hesse.

"He and Mr. Banes are on their way downtown. Good luck."

Larry vanished out the door and into his waiting Chrysler without a good-bye or a thank you. "Yeah, you're welcome," Louise muttered after him.

The all-important meeting with the FDA Review Board had been going on for two and a half hours, and Alex was getting very nervous. He sweated as he read from his notes in a stiff monotone, and the little glasses he wore were fogging up. Dr. Alexander Hesse's natural habitat was the laboratory, and he was always very ill-at-ease when speaking in public. The papers in his fingers rattled as his hands shook. Nevertheless, he believed with all his heart in the effectiveness of Expectane, a drug that would genuinely help expectant mothers carry their babies to term by reinforcing the fertilized egg's attachment. It enabled the developing fetus to hang on tight and not be rejected by the mother's body.

Alex Hesse was well aware—and even Larry Arbogast was aware, although he would not admit the possibility out loud—that most applications to the Food and Drug Administration for clinical trials on humans were turned down. That meant the end of the experimental drug right there. No matter how good the lab results looked on paper, no matter how effective it appeared to be on laboratory animals, the FDA was very picky where human testing was concerned.

What if the drug had toxic side effects? What if it were less effective in humans than in white rats or primates? Or suppose that the new drug would simply be too expensive to produce in useful quantities? Those were only some of the questions the FDA would be looking at before it gave Expectane the green light for testing on women.

The series of FDA meetings and conventions, including the Drug Review Board, was held in one of the city's large downtown hotels. The nine members of the review board sat at a long table, microphones in front of them for questioning, and each with an identical sheaf of papers at his or her fingertips—all the data and test results on Expectane. They had complete reports of Dr. Alexander Hesse's research and testing on primates, facts and figures, plus a proposal for human testing—how many women would be involved in the protocol, and exhaustive detailing of how Dr. Hesse planned to conduct the trials. The data in the papers also included the criteria for selecting the women for the study, and what health and safety precautions would be taken in the testing. There were separate breakdowns for the short-term phase of the testing and the long-term phase. The FDA was very rigorous in what it needed to know to give

10

consent for clinical trials, but Alex had, as usual, been very thorough in his answers.

"In testing the drug on chimpanzees with a history of miscarriages," continued Alex, "I found conclusively that in every instance the side effects observed were consistent with behavioral and metabolic changes in the subjects undergoing *un*assisted pregnancies. Nausea, appetite fluctuation, mood swings, irritability—"

Whoa. The dweeb was talking about negative side effects. Dropping the pencil with which he had been fidgeting impatiently, Larry Arbogast scrambled to his feet and took over. "In other words," he said glibly, "completely normal Lamb-Chop's-got-a-bun-in-the-oven type behavior. I'm telling you, this drug *really* works."

Larry grinned confidently, winking at the committee, which was made up of eight men and only one woman. A couple of the men chuckled in response to Larry's jest, and the lone committee woman shot them a look of contempt, which effectively silenced them.

Alex couldn't help a grimace that expressed his displeasure at his partner's unprofessional vulgarity, and resumed his address to the board.

"Madam Chairperson, gentlemen. The drug Expectane has been shown to be a safe, effective compound for assisting tissue adherence in miscarriage-prone female reproductive systems. We respectfully request the board's approval to carry on into an invasive human protocol."

An invasive human protocol? Was he nuts, using terms like that in front of the FDA? Larry leapt to his feet again. "You've got to let us try this on real women, women in *need*." He pitched his emotional harangue directly at the chairwoman. "Our sisters . . . our daughters—"

Alex heaved a deep sigh, exasperated; Larry's histrionics embarrassed him. In fact, they were also too much for the beleaguered chair.

"Dr. Arbogast—" she protested, but Larry was not to be stopped. He was on a roll.

"The *millions* who look longingly at a gurgling, precious infant and cry, 'Oh, but not for me—'"

"Dr. Arbogast!"

"Ma'am?" Larry's large, round brown eyes were two innocent pools of decorum.

"This is an FDA hearing, not a telethon," the chairwoman said dismissively. "We have all the information we need. Thank you."

Larry shrugged and sat down, but Noah Banes stood up in his place. "As director of Leland University Biotechnology Research Center," he proclaimed self-importantly, "and on behalf of my esteemed colleagues, thank you for your consideration."

It was over. The dice had been thrown; the button had been pushed; the wheel was spinning; the future of Expectane was now in the hands of the federal government's regulatory agency. Without human testing it would be impossible to market the drug, and no pharmaceutical company would touch it, let alone give the developers fistfuls of money. As Banes, Hesse, and Arbogast got off the hotel elevator into the street-floor lobby, all three men were talking at once.

"I'm telling you, it went *fine,*" insisted Larry.

"The chairwoman thought you were an idiot," Alex said glumly.

"She thought I was *committed,*" Larry retorted.

"It was agreed that I would do the presentation," Alex pointed out, his large brow furrowed.

"Look, it's *my* development money on the line here," Larry pointed out.

"*And* the university's," chimed in Banes.

"And *I'm* not worried," finished Larry. "So what's your problem?"

"It's your money, it's my *life*," Alex said hotly.

"Let's not bicker," Noah Banes said smoothly. "Yea or nay, we'll continue to support you. The work will go on."

Driving home in his Jeep, Alex couldn't shake the feelings of gloom that hung over him. Had he done his best at the hearing? Had he been credible enough? Had he convinced the board to let them go ahead with testing on humans? He had worked so hard on Expectane, had invested so much of his life and his future in the drug. To think that there was even a remote possibility that the FDA wouldn't allow Expectane to be tested on women filled Alex with foreboding. What would he do then? Where would he go next? Although the field of genetic engineering was only just beginning to explode, another project like Expectane would be hard to come by.

It was the perfect drug. Women who wanted to have babies but couldn't carry to term would, with Expectane, become happy mothers. Larry Arbogast might behave like a buffoon sometimes, but he hadn't been off the mark in what he told the FDA. There *were* millions of women who now believed that a precious baby was "oh, not for me."

Alex felt gloomy as he climbed the stairs to his apartment, gloomy as he spent the evening quietly going over his research notes, gloomy as he changed into clean pajamas, gloomy as he brushed his teeth and washed his face, gloomy as he made himself his nightly cup of hot cocoa in his tiny kitchen, gloomy as he climbed into bed and settled himself down among his pillows, gloomy as he picked up his remote control and aimed the clicker at the television set at the foot of his bed. Only the sight of the Weather Channel seemed to cheer Alex up a little, and he sipped his cocoa and watched his favorite program, the worldwide meteorology reports, until at last he was sleepy enough to switch off the light.

Dr. Lawrence Arbogast, on the other hand, was not at all gloomy. He was rarely if ever gloomy. Life was too short and too filled with opportunity, and if it didn't willingly come your way, you went out and tackled it, roped it, tied it, and dragged opportunity back to your cave. Larry had a successful practice, an excellent reputation, and an enviable track record in bringing fertility to infertile couples who desperately wanted children and could afford his professional services. He enjoyed his work, although he enjoyed even more the money The Fertility Center brought in. Larry had a good life, or at least, he had just about everything that an almost-seven-figure income could give him.

What he didn't have was a wife. His lovely wife Angela was now his lovely former wife, and the recipient of a generous alimony extracted from a kicking and screaming Larry Arbogast by a shrewd divorce lawyer and a compliant judge. For a while there, Larry held a grudge—he would curse quite colorfully and grind his molars together whenever he wrote the monthly check to Angela—but then he found the solution. He simply raised his patient fees and earned the difference back in no time. Then he almost stopped holding a grudge against Angela. See, if you knew what you were doing, you'd always come out on top.

Dr. Arbogast was with the Lanzarottas in the Mastubatorium when Louise came looking for him with her news. Larry was very proud of the Mastubatorium— although at the Center they never called it that in front of the clients; they always referred to it publicly as "the privacy room," and among themselves as "the nookie nook." The room didn't look at all clinical, but was arranged like a cozy living room, down to the wide daybed, the fireplace, and the TV/VCR with its complement of skin books, like *Penthouse,* and erotic videotapes. Larry wouldn't have minded spending time in there himself. But it was the Lanzarottas who were here for his help. Poor Mr. Lanzarotta had been, in his own words, "shooting blanks."

"I think you'll find this very comfortable," said Larry, handing Mrs. Lanzarotta a specimen cup. "We've got most of the popular magazines, a nice selection of videocassettes. So relax, take your time, just give it to Louise when you're finished. What do we say?" He cocked an ear for the response.

"He's loaded for bear and his aim is true," Mrs. Lanzarotta parroted stoutly.

Larry grinned broadly. "That's it! Enjoy!" He closed the door behind him and had started back down the hall toward the examining room when Louise came scurrying toward him from the other direction.

"Dr. Arbogast, your ex-wife's in your office. She says she won't leave until she sees you."

Angela? What the hell did she want? Probably another cockamamie project she wanted him to finance, like that art gallery that sold bidets decorated with animal antlers, and went belly-up in six months, taking a hundred grand of fertility money with it. Well, no way this time.

"Hi, Angela," Larry said brusquely as he stalked into his office. "What are you doing here?"

Petite and pretty, Angela Arbogast was about forty years old, slim and wide-eyed, although now her brows were drawn tightly together as she paced back and forth on the carpet, clearly agitated.

"Larry, I have something very important to tell you. Maybe you should sit down."

Sit down? This was gonna cost a bundle. "Angela, I'm busy!" Larry said, exasperated. "I don't have time to sit down."

"Larry, I'm pregnant!"

He sat down. The news caught Larry Arbogast off guard, and he was totally flabbergasted. "Really? That's . . . that's *wonderful!* Are you sure?"

Angela's hands were gripped together so tightly that the blood was drained from them and even her wrists were pale white. "Yes," she said shortly.

"How far along?"

"Seven weeks, give or take."

Seven weeks . . . let's see . . . Larry did some calculations in his head. "The night of the Kellman wedding?"

The lines around Angela's mouth cut even deeper as she shook her head mutely, tight-lipped.

"But that's the only time we did it in the last—" Larry broke off, suddenly realizing what her silence was telling him. The baby wasn't his; it was another man's. "Oh."

He wasn't one who did a lot of soul-searching; in truth, Larry Arbogast's glibness and sharp wit were a shell he had built around his emotions to contain them and keep his feelings from getting in his way as he ricocheted through life. But the shell cracked a bit now, and he was surprised at just how hurt he was feeling. After all, Angela was his *ex*-wife, as his checkbook stubs proved every month. What business was it of his if she went out and got herself knocked up?

"He was in and out of my life very quickly," she said in a low tone, not looking directly at him.

"Not quickly enough, apparently. He *who*?"

Angela shook her head. "It's not important."

"Does he know?"

"Not yet."

Larry took another stab at it. "Are you *sure* it's not mine?" he asked hopefully.

Now Angela looked fully at him, her huge eyes a little sad. "Larry," she said gently, "all the years we tried. You think one night, by *accident* . . . ?"

Irony gave Dr. Lawrence Arbogast another kick in the head with her booted foot. The co-owner of The Fertility Center, who had brought fertility to thousands, was a blanks-shooter. Physician, heal thyself. "Well, maybe one of mine bribed his way in or something . . ."

Angela smiled a little bitterly. "You should be happy it's not yours. I mean, we didn't get divorced because we were making each other so *happy*."

The intercom on his desk buzzed, but Larry ignored it. "Yeah, I guess you're right." He was clearly disappointed, but in true Larry Arbogast style he rallied. "So what do you want from me, Angela?"

"I want you to be my doctor."

This was more than he had bargained for. Much more, in fact, than he was willing to deal with. Angela, pregnant. Angela, here in his office as his patient, client, whatever—absolutely not. That would be way too close for comfort. He'd nip this in the bud right now. Larry shook his head vehemently. "No way. Dr. Fleming's perfectly capable."

"Dr. Fleming's a *hippie*!" Angela protested. "Larry, I want the best. Who's better than you?"

"Thank you, Angela." Despite himself, Larry felt a stab of satisfaction. He always loved hearing that he was the best. "But I couldn't even if I wanted to. We're related—"

"Dr. Arbogast?" Louise called from the outer office, now abandoning the intercom and knocking at the door.

"Not since the divorce," Angela said earnestly. "It's okay, I checked with the AMA. Please? I'm begging you!" It was obvious that she was serious in her request, although she had no idea how uncomfortable her request was making Larry feel.

"Dr. Arbogast!" Louise's voice held a real urgency.

"In a *minute*!" Larry yelled back impatiently. "No, Angela. Final. End of story. No can do. I'll ask Ned if he's got room for you. If there's anyone better than me, it's him."

"Ned Sneller?" Now it was Angela's turn to shake her head vehemently. "Forget it! He *looks* at me, Larry—"

But Larry was no longer listening. He opened his office door and barked at Louise. "What!?"

"Noah Banes on one. He says it's important."

"Even when we were married, he looked at me." Angela made another vain try to capture her ex-husband's attention.

Larry snatched up the phone and barked into it. "Banes." It was the last syllable he was able to get out before a tirade erupted on the other end of the line. He listened wordlessly, his face turning pale. All he gathered from the roiling spate of angry words was that Alex, the big dweeb, was doing something very stupid. When he spoke again at last, his voice held alarm. "I'm on my way over."

Slamming down the phone, Larry headed for the door at an anxious trot. Just before he disappeared, he gave one last, fleeting thought to Angela.

"Ned Sneller," he said to her. "Got the touch of a safecracker." He wiggled his pudgy little fingers delicately in the air, pantomiming the precise maneuvers of a world-class safecracker. Then, muttering angry curses at the big dweeb, he rushed out to his car.

Chapter Two

Diana

In his customary calm and methodical way, Dr. Alexander Hesse went on with his packing, while outside the locked door of his first-floor laboratory at the Lufkin Center all hell was breaking loose. Oblivious to the commotion, Alex continued to place his files carefully into a deep cardboard box, while Alice, his lab assistant, quietly packed his well-wrapped laboratory equipment into wooden crates.

Alex's life was coming apart, but you would never have guessed it from his expressionless face. He always confronted the ups and downs of fickle fortune with stoicism, keeping his feelings hidden in a calm-faced silence. That was another significant way that Dr. Hesse was the total opposite of Larry Arbogast, who concealed his feelings behind a waterfall of often mindless chatter.

The pounding on the locked door increased, and the angry voices in the corridor escalated both in vigor and in tone. They were really getting mad out there.

"Dr. Hesse? This is totally unacceptable behavior," shouted Noah Banes. "Please open this door—now!" At the sound of his icy voice, Minnie and Moe scurried back and forth in their cages, agitated.

But Alex paid the voice no attention. He was completely focused—as he knew how to be—on his packing, and he preserved his air of calm resignation. In the corridor outside, a milling knot of security guards and custodians were gathered in front of the large locked doors to the lab, banging on them with their fists. Now Noah Banes stepped up to the doors.

"Dr. Hesse, Banes here," he announced sonorously. "Let reason rule the day. Open up, now."

There was no reply from inside. After a moment, Banes nodded to two custodians, who began hammering at the hinge bolts of the doors, preparing to remove them by force.

The hammering made the chimpanzees whimper in fear. Alex spoke gently to them. "I will miss you most of all." To Alice he said, "I wish they would go away."

Alice raised her voice to the enemy in the corridor. "He wishes you would go away."

Larry Arbogast dashed into the Lufkin Center and came tearing down the corridor, dodging movers and equipment, heading for the commotion at the far end of the hall. "Banes!" he yelled. "What the hell's going on?!"

A tall figure detached itself from the knot and turned to greet him. "Arbogast, hey. Good news and bad news. FDA decision, *wicked* bad news."

Larry gasped and blanched. "They turned us down?!"

"I'm afraid so," Banes said smoothly. "And the review board's decided to terminate your project. Sorry. Lab space is tight, money's even tighter."

"Please, Banes, cut me some slack," begged Larry, the sweat glistening on his brow and his balding scalp. "I've got three hundred grand in this drug." What the hell ever happened to *Yea or nay, we'll continue to support you. The work will go on*?

Banes smiled coldly, his face bland. "Would that I could, Doctor. But my hands are tied, sorry. Blame it on the board."

"You're *head* of the board!" Larry protested in anguish, his voice rising in an agonized squeak.

Banes shrugged without changing his frozen expression. "Yes, I am. Rock and a hard place."

With a loud pinging noise, a hinge pin went flying. The custodians were making progress on the doors.

"So what's the good news?" Larry demanded sourly.

Now Noah Banes's aloof eyes lit up with something like enthusiasm. "I've landed Dr. Diana Reddin and her Ovum Cryogenics Project."

"Freezing eggs? Big deal!" snarled Larry.

"Now, now, no sour grapes." Banes turned back to the custodians. "How're those doors coming?"

At this very moment, the aforementioned Dr. Diana Reddin was right outside the open service entrance doors of Lufkin Center, a clipboard in her hand, standing at bottom of the ramp leading up to a large state-of-the-art moving van. She was supervising—or trying to—a pair of exasperated movers. All she had succeeded in doing so far was get in the way.

Let us take a moment to consider the eminent research scientist Dr. Diana Reddin, for she is a person well worth considering. An Englishwoman in her middle thirties, Diana speaks with a cultivated Oxbridge accent not unlike Her Majesty the Queen's, an accent she was born to and which she reinforced at Cambridge in her university years.

Tall, thin, with long legs and arms and a thick mop of

light brown hair that turns blond under the rays of the summer sun, Diana has a classic, serious, even somewhat severe face that is softened by a pair of large blue eyes and is made suddenly beautiful whenever she smiles her broad and radiant smile.

She wasn't smiling now. Dr. Diana Reddin was dithering around anxiously, getting into the movers' path, hindering their work, and pissing them off no end. The specialized equipment-moving van, rented for $500 an hour, had already been almost completely disburdened of its scientific equipment, despite Diana's interference. What remained to be moved was a large, wheeled, stainless steel locker, which the movers now rolled to the top of the ramp, preparing to bring it down to the street and into the Lufkin Center. The locker was wrapped in padded movers' packing quilts and plastered with labels reading "Caution—Nitrogen" and "Contents Very Fragile." This freezer locker was the linchpin of Dr. Reddin's Ovum Cryogenics Project, to which her life was completely devoted.

At the sight of it, Diana became even more anxious. "Please be *extremely* careful with that," she urged.

Sal, the larger of the two moving men, growled down at her. "Lady, if I hear that one more time out of you—"

With a jerky movement, Diana tried to hoist herself onto the back of the van. "You can't be up here, ma'am," cautioned Eddie, the other mover. "Union rules."

Diana shook her head. "I have to set the levelers for the incline." She grabbed a nearby handle to pull herself up, but it was no ordinary hand grip, it was the hydraulic control for the ramp. As Diana put her weight on it, the ramp began rising up. Instantly the movers jumped toward her, and the locker rolled forward a couple of feet and stopped.

"Whoopsie daisy! Sorry!" Having reached the top of the ramp, Diana giggled nervously. She lifted the lever back into position, and the ramp, released, dropped sharply down, hitting the sidewalk. The locker lurched forward and began to roll down the slope.

"*No!*" yelled Diana and both moving men simultaneously. "My babies!!" shrieked Diana, and she struggled to hold the steel locker back. But it was already too late. Gaining momentum, it rolled down the ramp, and Diana did the only thing she could think of. She took a flying leap and threw herself on top of the locker.

The addition of her weight only increased its speed, and the steel locker hurtled off the ramp and sped across the sidewalk and in through the open doors of the Lufkin Center. Once it hit the polished floor of the corridor, the locker, carrying Diana as its passenger, rolled smoothly and very swiftly along, heading straight for Banes, Larry, the workmen, and the locked doors of Dr. Alexander Hesse's laboratory.

"Help!!" yelled Diana at the top of her lungs. "I mean it!!!"

At her cry, Larry and Banes turned in astonishment. They saw a bizarre juggernaut hurtling toward them, evidently piloted by a wide-eyed, yelling woman. There was no time for them to figure out what the hell was happening; there was only time for them to scramble the hell out of her way. At the very moment that she reached the threshhold of Alex's lab, the custodians got the last hinge pins out and took the doors off. The unimpeded locker, with Diana aboard, barreled straight through the open doorway and into the laboratory.

Alex Hesse saw the locker heading toward him at top speed, and his lightning reflexes took over. He dropped the box he was packing, threw himself in the path of the steel juggernaut, and with amazing strength stopped it with his body. Diana pitched forward, slid off the top, and fell into Alex's arms. With her on top of him, Alex toppled to the floor.

For a moment they lay there, nose to nose. Diana saw a serious face, not exactly handsome, but interesting, intelligent, very strong and masculine. Alex saw a serious face, not conventionally pretty, but with superb bone structure and wide blue eyes under a broad, intelligent brow.

"I could just *kiss* you!" Diana declared to her hero.

"That won't be necess—"

But it was too late. Diana mashed her face against his, kissing him hard, pushing his nose to one side. At last she came up for air. Alex was regarding her with a startled, uncomfortable expression. It hadn't been an unpleasant experience for him . . . not by any means . . . but this strange woman's impulsiveness had caught him off guard.

Seeing Alex's discomfort, Diana took it wrong. It hadn't been much of a kiss, she thought. "Sorry," she said, flustered, "guess I'm a bit out of practice."

Alex was equally flustered. "Excuse me," he said, "I must finish packing." Yet neither one of them moved. They were still lying on the floor, with Diana on top of Alex.

By now Noah Banes and Larry Arbogast were in the laboratory. "Are you all right?" Banes asked solicitously, hovering over Diana.

She got quickly to her feet, accidentally treading on Alex's hand. Alex uttered a small grunt of pain, but it went unnoticed in the excitement surrounding Diana. "Well, yes, *I'm* fine, but . . ."

Diana tore the padding off the freezer locker and pushed a switch. The vacuum released with a hiss, and the top of the locker opened with a hydraulic whoosh. A mist formed by the nitrogen coolant rose from the locker, and as if by magic, a gridded tray rose up out of the mist, revealing rows of steel canisters holding suspended, capped, and labeled test tubes.

Alex got up slowly and rather painfully, and quietly resumed his packing. Nobody paid any attention to him. Banes and Larry were peering over Diana's shoulder as she carefully checked the test tubes.

"Thank God, they're all right."

"Frozen eggs, huh?" asked Larry.

Diana smiled brightly and proudly. "Yes. I call it the dairy section. And if it weren't for the heedless bravery of—" She looked around for Alex Hesse, but he was no longer in the laboratory. "He's leaving? He's gone," she finished, disappointed.

They all looked around, puzzled. "Hesse?" called Larry.

"Dr. Hesse has left the building," said his lab assistant, Alice, stiffly.

Diana had a sudden unpleasant revelation. "This is *his* laboratory, isn't it?"

"Was," said Larry sourly, and he left abruptly, taking off after Alex.

"Do you like it?" asked Banes solicitously.

"Well, yes, but I didn't want to displace anyb—"

"You're not," Banes assured her briefly. He turned to the security guards. "Take the chimps back to the primate lab. We won't be needing them anymore." Now he turned his flattering attention back to his new prize catch, the well-known British scientist who just might bring the university its Nobel Prize. "I was thinking of repainting in here, a soft blue perhaps, to go with your eyes . . ."

A taxicab was idling in front of Alex Hesse's apartment building when Larry Arbogast pulled up in his Chrysler. He jumped out of the car and ran into the building. Reaching Alex's apartment, he knocked at the door, but it was unlocked and swung open under Larry's insistent rapping.

There was a suitcase standing at the door, and as Larry entered and looked around, Alex was just coming out of the bedroom with two more suitcases in his large hands.

"Hesse?! Where are you going?"

Alex's expression didn't change. "I'm flying to Paris and starting over. Good-bye," he said without emotion.

Larry felt a chilly hand clutching at his heart. "You're running out on me? I don't believe this!" His tone changed from indignation to pleading. "Listen, Hesse, we're *partners* in this! You can't just up and leave!"

Alex reached for the third suitcase, but Larry beat him to it with surprising agility, and planted his plump, determined little rump on it.

"You'll make your money back," Alex said. "I have no lab, no funding, no future here. Now get off my bag."

For a moment, the two men grappled for the bag, but it was—given their relative sizes and strengths—an unequal contest, and within seconds Alex was heading out his apartment door with three suitcases. But Larry remained attached to his heels like a little terrier dog, trying without success to keep Alex from loading his bags into the taxicab's trunk.

"Hold on a minute, will you? What about all the people you'd be leaving behind?" For a second, no name came to mind, then Larry Arbogast had an inspiration. "Your girlfriend! What's her name again?"

"Sasha?"

"Sasha, yeah!" Larry brightened. "You want to break that pretty little heart?"

"She moved to Santa Fe with my best friend Nigel, three months ago."

Larry didn't miss a beat. "Ah, you're better off." Then he continued, undaunted. "What about your colleagues? I know for a *fact* that your skill and dedication is an *inspiration* to everyone. They'd be lost without you."

For the first time, Alex permitted a tinge of bitterness to color his words. "Yes, they'll have to find someone else to mimic over coffee in the lounge." The luggage was loaded, and now Alex climbed into the cab.

"Come on . . . they don't . . . that's not true," Larry stammered. It *was* true, but Larry was surprised to learn that Alex was actually aware of his colleagues' mockery. He'd never given a sign.

"I'm not well liked," Alex said matter-of-factly.

"*I* like you!" Larry protested.

"No, you don't. Good-bye." The cab drove off. Larry ran for his car, and sped off after him, in the direction of the airport.

The cab stopped for a red light at a busy intersection. The Chrysler pulled up next to it, and Larry made frantic motions for Alex to lower his window. Irritated, Alex rolled the window down.

"The chimps, Minnie and Moe," Larry called, possessed by a new idea born of his desperation.

"What about the chimps?" demanded Alex.

Now that he had Hesse's attention, Larry launched into his histrionics, drawing on all of his talent for evoking an emotion in his hearer. "*They* like you! They *love* you! And did any guy ever have more loyal friends? Giving everything, asking nothing in return but love and bananas—"

"Don't patronize me," Alex interrupted wearily.

"That Moe!" continued Larry, on a roll. "Remember when you ran the Expectane protocol on him? We had him *pregnant,* he was *miserable,* but never once did he look at you with anything but trust in those big brown—"

Larry Arbogast broke off, as a sudden idea flashed across his brain, an idea so daring, so unexpected, that it literally took his breath away. Only once in a lifetime is it given to anybody to have an idea as great, as earth-shattering, as potentially profitable as this one. He stared at Alex, his eyes wide.

Alex stared back, a little confused. Larry didn't often stop talking unless he was firmly interrupted. And why was he looking at him like that, so . . . speculatively? But before Alex Hess had time to wonder about it, the light changed to green and the cab took off again. Alex turned to look out of the back window.

Larry was still sitting in the light, looking somewhat dazed. He was in a fog of revelation, thinking furiously. Behind him, horns began to honk loudly and angrily, as impatient drivers shouted at him and cursed him for sitting in the middle of the intersection at a green light, holding up the flow of traffic. Larry snapped out of his fog and peeled off, burning rubber in his pursuit of Alex's taxi. Now as never before he needed the big dweeb.

Larry Arbogast caught up with Alex Hesse at San Francisco Airport, just as Alex was leaving the Continental Airlines counter, tucking his tickets and passport into his jacket pocket. "I talked to my guy at Lyndon Pharmaceuticals," he said in a confidential loud whisper, as though continuing the conversation they were having at the intersection. "You know, that Canadian company?"

"Larry, *good-bye!*" Alex said firmly, scowling.

"They're willing to kick in some additional funding provided we find a volunteer for the Expectane protocol."

Alex eyed him suspiciously. "We can't do the protocol without FDA approval."

Larry made a gesture of brushing aside the obvious. "We can if we don't *tell* the FDA. Are we going to let some Washington bureaucrats stand in the way of progress?"

Alex shot Larry a look of dismissal. "What woman's going to take an unapproved drug when she's pregnant?" he demanded.

"Who says we *need* a woman?" retorted Larry with a significant raise of his eyebrow.

They had reached the security scanners. Alex showed the guard his ticket and boarding pass and passed through the scanners. He turned back to Larry. "What are you talking about?"

Larry's little round face lit up with the light of inspiration. This was a beauty idea, a million-dollar concept. "The new experiment wouldn't have to identify the subject's *sex*. Just the human tissue reactives!" He took a step closer to Alex. "Remember Moe? He went five months to term!"

Alex gasped and his eyes went wide as Larry's meaning sank in. "You mean, test it on a *man*?"

Larry smiled blandly, spreading his hands out, palms up. "Why not? You allergic to anything?"

"*Me?!* You're nuts." Alex backed away from Larry, shaking his head in disbelief.

Larry took another step forward, but the security guard stopped him. "Only ticketed passengers with boarding passes beyond this point."

Alex moved forward toward the gate, still shaking his head. What a flake that Larry Arbogast was.

"Hesse, wait! Hear me out!"

But Alex didn't turn. There was only one thing to do, and Larry did it, trotting back to the Continental Airlines ticket counter, waving his gold credit card. He made a quick and expensive purchase of one of the only two remaining San Francisco-to-Paris tickets and rushed back to the departure gate, flashing his boarding pass.

The airline had called the flight and already begun boarding. Larry pushed his determined way through and around the other passengers until he reached Alex Hesse's side as Alex was passing through the tunnel that led from the gate to the airplane door. Alex was not at all happy to see him, but Larry didn't care. He just picked up his spiel where he had left off, except that now he was out of breath from all the dashing around and had to gasp out his words.

"You wouldn't be *pregnant* pregnant. Sort of a guest host situation," he explained in an undertone, so the other passengers wouldn't overhear. "We fertilize an egg and implant it in your peritoneal cavity, dose you with the Expectane. Tiny thing, grain of rice, you carry it through the first trimester, we've got our data—boom, it's over."

The flight attendant checked Alex's boarding pass. "Hi, how areya," said Larry with a grin, showing his.

"Four-A, to your right," the flight attendant told Alex. She glanced at Larry's pass. "Fifty-one-F, all the way back."

They moved inside the 747, and Alex headed for his seat in the forward cabin. "First class, huh?" Larry said pointedly. "Good for you."

"It's not possible, it's not natural, and I'm not interested," Alex said shortly but definitely. He found his place, a window seat next to a young, pretty mother holding a beautiful infant.

"Guess I had you wrong, Hesse," Larry said sharply. "I took you for a *scientist*."

"I *am* a scientist." Alex climbed over mother and daughter and settled into his seat.

"Oh, yeah? Well, where's your *vision*? Jenner infected himself with smallpox to test his vaccine."

There was a point to Larry's words that took Alex by surprise and gave him pause. "Jenner, yes," he said thoughtfully.

"Well, why not *you*?" Larry pressed his point, warming to his subject, waving his arm expansively. "Is it possible—who knows? Natural? So what? Good science? You bet! Come and claim your place in the pantheon!"

Alex wasn't moved by Larry's phoney dramatic eloquence, but the phrase "good science" struck a nerve in the core of him. He looked at the beautiful little baby in the seat next to him, and the infant cooed happily at him. He gave a thought to Expectane, and the good it could do for so many if it were marketed. Other women, previously doomed to barrenness, could become mothers of infants like this.

"You're just trying to manipulate me," he accused.

"Yes, I am," Larry admitted cheerfully. "So what? Opportunity's knocking *here*. Opportunity for *greatness*. Now, are you going to answer the door, or always regret what might have been?"

There was a loud *ding,* and the "Fasten Seat Belt" light flashed on. The flight attendant came up behind Larry. "Excuse me, sir, I'll have to ask you to take your seat."

It was fish-or-cut-bait time. Desperation City. This plane would be on its way to Paris in less than five minutes, and Larry Arbogast didn't speak French.

"Cards on the table," he said with finality. "I don't like you any more than you like me. You've got all the warmth and charm of a wall-eyed pike, and if we weren't partners . . . The point is, we *are* partners, and we're on the verge of something *fantastic* here, something *important,* and I need you to see it through with me, okay? There's no one else. I need you." He let out his breath, having said everything he could to convince Alex that his scheme was feasible.

It was the naked truth, the only time that Alex had ever heard Larry speak it. Despite his doubts, he was impressed. The young mother in the next seat turned to him and said in a charming French accent, "Your friend could really use your help." At the same time, the flight attendant was growing increasingly impatient.

34

"Sir," she said to Larry, "You're going to *have* to take your seat."

Larry looked imploringly at Alex. "Please don't make me fly all the way to Paris! In coach!?"

Alex sighed, defeated. He wondered briefly whether his suitcases would have a good time in Paris and whether he'd ever see his luggage again. He looked at Larry Arbogast grinning happily and hoped that Larry was right. Only a seat in the pantheon of great scientists would be worth what he was agreeing to.

"It *could* work," he said slowly, as he and Larry left the airport. He'd been giving it thought: why shouldn't it work? The procedure itself was fairly simple. A human egg fertilized in vitro would be implanted into his abdominal cavity, where it would grow on and take nourishment from the abdominal covering, the omentum. All he'd have to do was to carry the developing embryo through the first trimester, only three months, and they'd have the data they needed on human testing.

"Yes, yes it could," agreed the jubilant Larry Arbogast. He resisted the overwhelming impulse to laugh out loud, hug himself, and jump up and down.

Alex's enthusiasm went up a notch. "What a leap forward it would be!" He was picturing the smiles on the faces of the couples who were desperate to become parents. He was picturing the articles in the most respected scientific journals. He was picturing the respect he would earn from his peers and colleagues.

"One giant leap for mankind." Larry's enthusiasm went up several notches. He was picturing the many, many zeros on the checks he would be receiving from Lyndon Pharmaceuticals.

"You're sure you can get an egg?" Alex asked.

"Leave it to me," Larry assured him confidently. He knew exactly where he could find eggs . . . dozens of eggs . . . carefully stored, capped, labeled, waiting . . .

Larry had counted on the Lufkin Center's forgetting or else not bothering to change the locks on Dr. Alexander Hesse's former laboratory; as Alex's partner, he had a key. He was right; his key worked perfectly, just as it always had. Using the sharp beam of a halogen flashlight for illumination, in the twinkling of an eye Larry had waltzed himself into the lab and made a beeline for Dr. Diana Reddin's precious Ovum Cryogenics Project, kept in nitrogen cold storage and housed in a steel freezer locker.

He flipped the switch that cracked the seal on the freezer lid, and the rack of test tubes rose up with a whoosh, in a covering of frozen nitrogen mist. Oh, boy, what riches! Larry chuckled exultantly.

"Eeny meeny miney mo . . . catch a baby by the toe . . ." The flashlight beam circled over the rack of eggs. Which to choose, oh, which to choose? Larry read some of the names typed on the labels. One appealed to him, and he lifted "Junior" from the rack. "C'mon, Junior, we're going for a ride."

Carefully, he placed the test tube with Junior in it into the zippered dry ice pack slung over his shoulder by a strap, and zipped it up. Mission accomplished. One egg, poached. Good gag, considering that Larry Arbogast had just been poaching on private property.

As he turned to go, Larry Arbogast's flashlight beam shone directly onto Dr. Diana Reddin, asleep at her desk, her head pillowed on a cheese-and-tomato sandwich. He jumped a foot in the air, and when the bright light woke her up, so did Diana. It would be a draw as to which of them was more startled by the unexpected sight of the other.

"Dr. Arbogast?" she asked, her brow furrowing in surprise.

"Dr. Reddin! What are you doing here?" Larry inched back from the freezer and unobtrusively shifted his dry ice bag behind him.

"Where? I don't know—where am I?" She seemed unaware that a slice of the sandwich cheese had left the sandwich and was now plastered to her cheek. "Oh, the lab. Yes, *my* lab. So what are *you* doing here?"

Good question. It needed a good answer. Larry thought fast, and talked even faster. "I . . . uh . . . It's like . . . when a ball player's traded, you know? Yeah. And he . . . uh . . . goes out to the ballpark, you know, alone, just him and his thoughts to . . . to . . . take a last look, memorizing the turf, the infield, the angles of the light . . ." He stopped babbling, hoping that he had made at least some sense, reached forward, and gently pulled the piece of cheese off Diana's face. Without the cheddar, she was a real looker, a very classy babe.

"Thank you," Diana said absently. Larry's less-than-glib explanation had left her just as puzzled as before. What *was* he doing here? "I thought you were a gynecologist."

"That's right, I am. By the way, do you have someone locally?"

"So what are you doing in this lab?" Diana Reddin was nothing if not persistent. She reminded Larry of Alex Hesse in her single-minded pursuit of information.

"Oh. See, I was partnered with Dr. Hesse on the

Expectane formula. Spent a lot of long nights here, I'll tell you. Lot of memories. Whew!"

He eyed her closely, and saw that Diana seemed to accept this explanation as somewhat more credible. A shape in the darkness caught his eye, and he saw Minnie and Moe, the chimpanzees, curled up asleep together in their cage. "Minnie and Moe, you kept them," Larry said.

"I couldn't very well turn out an expectant mother, now could I?" countered Diana. But in fact she was glad of the chimps' company; it was often lonely, working by oneself in a laboratory.

"Alex will be very happy."

Diana nibbled at her lower lip. "I get the feeling that Dr. Hesse blames me for the loss of his facility." She sounded uncomfortable.

Larry shrugged. "He did take it kind of hard, but I don't think it's anything too personal. He's just kind of chronically cranky."

"Well, I hate to see anyone's work go unfinished because of budget constraints. Please tell him I'm happy to help out with lab time and materials. I'm sure we could even spare a little room, if he's amenable to sharing . . ."

Larry leapt in quickly. Time, materials, space—it was an unexpected bonanza. "That would be extremely generous and more helpful than you can imagine," he said, successfully hiding his glee. He held out his hand to Diana, and she shook it, while he checked out the ring finger on her left hand. "Is there a *Mister* Dr. Reddin?" he asked archly.

"No," said Diana shortly.

He looked up coyly into her face, which was many inches above his. "Dinner sometime?"

"No. Good night, Dr. Arbogast."

Larry slunk out of the laboratory with mixed feelings. He had gotten what he'd come for—the egg. He had Junior. He'd gotten more than he'd hoped for—Diana's offer of lab space and facilities for Alex. But as to scoring with Dr. Diana Reddin—to retain Larry Arbogast's own baseball metaphor, he hadn't even come up to bat.

Chapter Three

Larry

The next step in the process was to make Junior the purloined egg fertile, and the logical sperm donor was Dr. Alexander Hesse, the "guest host." After Larry phone Alex to tell him that he had a suitable egg, Alex turned up by arrangement at The Fertility Center. It was late the same night; the lights were out and the doors locked when Larry arrived to open up. Alex and Larry were the only two at the Center. What they were doing there at that hour was nobody's business except theirs . . . and Junior's.

It goes without saying that Larry Arbogast did not inform Alex—or anybody—that he had actually stolen the egg from Dr. Diana Reddin's Ovum Cryogenics Project, or that the egg had been labeled "Junior." If Alex Hesse wished to presume that the egg had been obtained by legitimate means, who was Larry Arbogast to disabuse him of that notion? And if Dr. Hesse asked no questions, Dr. Arbogast was surely not obligated to provide him with answers.

What Larry did provide Alex with was a specimen cup and an introduction to the famous Mastubatorium, which Alex regarded with an air of gloomy distaste. Such frills and furbelows were loathesome to him, just sugar coating on what should be strictly scientific. On going inside,

Alex eyeballed the girlie magazines and the titles on the XXX-rated videos, and snorted in contempt. As usual, he was taking all of this very seriously, and his interest was purely scientific. Larry closed the door behind him to give Alex privacy, and paced back and forth outside the Mastubatorium, waiting for the specimen cup and its filler to emerge. A great deal—a fortune, in fact—was riding on that little cup.

In much less time than Larry had expected, Alex came out of the room, still wearing an expression of distaste, and handed his partner the specimen cup without looking at him. Suppressing a little crow of triumph, Larry led the way to the clinic's laboratory, and switched on the light inside the electron microscope. Junior was already waiting in her petri dish on the microscope stage under the lens. Larry had carefully disposed of the "evidence"— Dr. Reddin's telltale freezer test tube with its name label. Now Junior had become a totally anonymous thawed-out ovum and was buffed and fluffed and ready for her blind date.

The reproductive technology of IVF—in vitro fertilization—is one of the medical miracles of this century. The term *in vitro* is Latin; it means "in glass" and refers to the glass petri dish in which Mr. Sperm meets Ms. Egg and the act of fertilization takes place. There's not a lot of privacy in the act; it's usually performed under a microscope. When the egg is fertilized and has divided into between four and eight cells, the ovum is introduced into its new home, the uterus—or, in the case of Dr. Alexander Hesse, the peritoneal cavity—there to grow into another human being.

The Fertility Center was well equipped to perform every kind of treatment for infertility, from a simple progesterone shot through the accepted surgeries—laparoscopy, hysteroscopy, and the fiber-optic surgery called endoscopy—all of which are designed to clear the uterus of fibroids or adhesions or endometriosis and prepare it for receiving a fertilized egg. In Alex's case, all that would be necessary was a simple IVF implantation by laparoscopic needle, plus Expectane therapy combined with hormone therapy to keep his abdominal lining thick enough to nourish the embryo before the formation of the placenta. The drug therapy would be continued after the placenta was formed, to reduce the risk of miscarriage.

With utmost delicacy surprising in such small, pudgy hands, Dr. Lawrence Arbogast punctured a hole in the outermost membrane of the egg, using a long, super-thin sterile needle. "Here we go," he muttered.

From another needle, Larry dispensed a few drops of Alex's viscous sperm into the petri dish and peered into the eyepiece of the microscope. He could see about fifty thousand miniscule sperm cells with tails wriggling around the much larger egg, drawn to it by that mysterious magnetism in nature called the reproductive process.

"Terrific mobility," said Larry exultantly under his breath, hunching over the scope with Alex hovering over him. "*Magnificent* count."

"What did you say?" asked Alex, who hadn't heard him clearly.

"Strong swimmers, big load."

Okay. Stage number one was completed; stage number two was to get the fertilized egg safely into Alex Hesse's body while it was still fresh. In women who participate in the process of in vitro fertilization, the egg is implanted

43

directly into the ovary, and the placenta forms around it. In the unique case of Alex, the egg would be implanted directly into the peritoneal lining of the abdominal cavity in a procedure termed a laparoscopy. Once infusions of Expectane and female hormones were added, the embryo would form its own placenta and grow, taking its nourishment directly from the omentum.

Theoretically, a pregnant male could carry a fetus to full term, nine months, and actually deliver the baby by means of cesarean section. But of course, that would not be the case with Alex here; only the first trimester would suffice as proof of Expectane's efficacy and safety. That was the agreement: three months and out.

Larry went to scrub up and dress in his surgical greens. In the well-equipped recovery room, Alex prepped himself, taking his shirt off to reveal a powerful musculature and very flat, taut belly, swabbing his abdomen with a sterilizing solution, and hooking himself up to the heart rate and blood pressure monitors. When Larry came back in wearing a hospital gown, cap, and mask and carrying a beaker, Alex was already sitting up on the examining table.

"Ready?" asked Larry.

"Read back the dosage."

Larry checked the label taped on the beaker. "Ten cc's Expectane, supplemented with one hundred milligrams progesterone."

Alex drank the solution down in one long gulp and lay back on the table. Larry positioned the ultrasound device, checked the image on the screen, and took up a very long laparoscopic needle. He approached the table, needle poised. "Here we go . . ."

Alex shut his eyes.

When he opened them again, he was in one of The Fertility Center's patient rooms, sitting up in bed dressed in a hospital gown. He felt wonderful, all warm and happy. Bubbly even. Larry Arbogast came in, and he, too, was smiling broadly and serenely. A pretty young nurse entered behind him, and she was smiling, too. Everybody was smiling; everybody was happy. Why was everybody so happy?

The nurse was carrying a bassinet and in the bassinet was a squalling baby. The nurse placed the bassinet on the bed next to Alex, and he looked down into it expectantly. And gasped in horror.

There, in the basket, was a tiny replica of himself, a completely miniaturized grown-up, even down to the little round glasses Alex wore when he worked. The replica was wearing a blue hospital bracelet on one wrist, and its bottom was dressed in diapers. It was crying lustily, but when it caught sight of Alex, the disconcerting squalling dwindled to a snuffle.

"Mama?" whimpered the infant, waving its arms imploringly at Alex.

Alex stared, flabbergasted.

Now the snuffling became a plea. *"Mama?!!"*

But Mama Alex was frozen, unable to respond. He could only stare, overwhelmed by the sight of his prodigious progeny, and even more overwhelmed by the misunderstanding of gender that was happening here.

"Maaaamaaaaa!!!" It was the infant's frightened cry of desperation, and it was meant for Alex to respond to with a mother's care.

Alex couldn't stand it. He clapped his hands over his ears and closed his eyes tightly to shut out the sight and sound of the baby he'd given birth to.

When he opened his eyes again, he sat up with a start, and looked around, disoriented. Alex found himself fully dressed on a frilly canopied bed, on a spread patterned with huge cabbage roses. In fact, cabbage roses appeared to be the prevailing motif here. The wallpaper, the carpeting, the chintz skirt on the vanity table, the chintz draperies at the windows—all added up to a veritable floral riot of cabbage roses. It was as though the interior designer Laura Ashley herself had whirled through here like a mad Victorian fairy godmother, waving a rose wand. Any hay fever sufferer trapped in this room would perish miserably.

Alex felt like a captive honeybee. He had no idea where he was or how he got here. "Larry? *Larry!!*" he yelled.

Larry Arbogast came trotting in. "Good morning!" he chirped cheerfully.

"Where am I?!" demanded Alex.

"My house. You're staying with me during the protocol, remember?"

Yes, he was starting to remember now. It was all beginning to come back to him. His own capitulation to Dr. Lawrence Arbogast's insane suggestion. Good science. The egg. The powerfully swimming sperm. The petri dish. The fertilization, the implantation with that humongous needle. His first ingestion of Expectane, the female hormones that were surging through him this very minute. Alex nodded vaguely, still groggy from last night's procedure, still trembling with the memory of that awful dream, that screaming infant who looked exactly like him, the baby who called him Mama. What a nightmare! Well, Alex had given his word. He couldn't go back on it now. Anyway, in just three months it would all be over.

Larry took a thermometer and a blood pressure cuff from the array of medical equipment laid out on the dresser top. He popped the thermometer into Alex's mouth, wrapped the cuff around Alex's upper arm, and began to pump it up.

Alex looked around at the room. "Mmmmmfffnnn," he commented, around the thermometer.

"My ex-wife's bedroom," answered Larry with pride. "Cheerful, huh? She decorated it herself. She had taste, gotta give her that."

"Nnnnflmmmm?" asked Alex.

"No, we didn't always have separate bedrooms. There are many stops along the road to divorce." Larry took a reading off the blood pressure monitor. "Blood pressure good." He reached over, took the thermometer out of Alex's mouth, and held it up to read it. "Ninety seven seven. Normal."

"I have to pee," Alex said urgently.

Larry handed him a specimen cup, saying, "Yeah, I'll need that, too." He followed Alex into the bathroom, which featured a shower curtain patterned with cabbage roses. There were cabbage roses on the towels and on the bath mat. Everything matched; everything made Alex's skin crawl. "We'll be running those tests at eight A.M. and again at ten P.M. every day. I've got a prenatal monitor and a blood screener ordered up, and we'll be tracking your progress at the nightly sessions."

"If you don't mind, I'd like some privacy," growled Alex. He really hated peeing in public.

"You got it, big guy," Larry said cheerfully. This was going to work out just fine. He had Alex under his personal supervision, and the protocol would go exactly according to plan; Larry was certain of it. One trimester and out. Then they'd all be richer than even Larry's wildest dreams, and where a big pile of money was concerned, Larry Arbogast's dreams were in wide-screen Technicolor.

"I'll analyze and collate the fluid samples at the lab every day, and we can chart our progress every Friday," called Alex from the bathroom.

Larry fetched a plastic case and a digital wristwatch from the dresser as Alex came out of the bathroom holding at arm's length his urine sample in the specimen cup. Larry took the sample and handed over the wristwatch.

Larry's voice was more clipped and efficient-sounding than Alex had ever heard it. "There's an alarm on it, set to go off every three hours, to remind you to take your medicine. There's individual doses of the Expectane-progesterone compound in the case. What d'you think— six times a day?"

"Yes," Alex said and nodded, "four-hour intervals."

Larry picked up an eyedropper and squeezed a couple of drops of testing solution into Alex's specimen. "How are you feeling?" he asked solicitously.

Alex considered the question. "I feel like I'm crazy to be doing this," he answered soberly.

Larry held out the specimen cup, grinning. The urine was bright blue. "You may be crazy, but you're also pregnant. Congratulations!"

The news hit Alex Hesse like a pile driver. It wasn't unexpected, and it was the natural outcome of last night's procedure, yet hearing it put flatly into words was almost shocking. The words took his delicate condition from the merely theoretical to the terrifyingly actual. He scarcely knew what to think. "Pregnant," he breathed, "I'm *pregnant.*"

He took a long look at himself in Angela Arbogast's full-length mirror. Alex didn't know what he expected to see, but it seemed to him he looked exactly the same as always. Pulling his shirt up, Alex studied his belly critically, turning this way and that, studying his image in the looking glass. His belly was flat and muscular and totally familiar. He pulled his shirt back down, relieved. Only one trimester and out.

It was a tight squeeze in the Lufkin Center laboratory. Present were Dr. Reddin and her two lab assistants, Arthur and Jenny, and now there was also Dr. Hesse and *his* lab assistant, Alice. Not to mention the large chimpanzee cage containing Minnie and Moe and their new baby, a tiny female who entranced the chimp parents and kept them busy playing with her for hours on end. Sometimes simply moving back and forth proved a logistical problem.

Yet in the three weeks since Alex had come to share Diana's lab, there had been no conflict between the two research scientists. This was because each of them was wrapped up totally in his or her own work, Diana on the Ovum Cryogenics Project, and Alex on . . . what?

He had never mentioned to Diana what he was working on, and she never thought to question him about it. She kept to her part of the lab, and he kept to his. They were alike, these two loners—private, scholarly, reticent, work-oriented. Each minded his or her own business. Not that they behaved uncivilly toward each other, not at all: it was just that both of them believed that a laboratory was a sacred precinct dedicated to scientific endeavor; it wasn't Club Med.

Alex had been granted a corner of the lab space, where he had set up his computer, and he was happy to be hunched intensely over the keyboard, typing away and checking the calibrations and calculations in the windows on the screen. Only now the 3-D graphic figure that turned slowly, showing a succession of front and side views, was not a chimpanzee, it was a human. The legend on the screen read "Three Weeks Impregnation." Dr. Hesse was monitoring his own test levels, using the data collected by Larry Arbogast from the nightly blood and urine screenings. While he worked, he kept rubbing at his chest in an unconscious gesture of discomfort.

Dr. Diana Reddin's project utilized more than one computer and several monitors, all of them busy showing complicated data charts and mysterious graphics, the import of which Diana was explaining carefully to her lab assistants, to brief them for the next phase of their work. "Embryo three is entering its four-to-six stage. Today we'll be extracting an eight-cell cluster and freezing it—" At the sound of a sudden groan, she broke off, startled.

Alex Hesse suddenly bolted to his feet, pushing his chair out of the way. Clapping one hand over his mouth, he lurched unsteadily in the direction of the bathroom. He was looking a little green. Concerned, Alice took a step toward him, but he waved her away, darting past her.

After the interruption, Diana continued with her briefing, picking up in mid-sentence. ". . . for the induced suspension and development arrest, looking for evidence of cryonic disruption of the DNA footprints and, if necessary, comparing the aberration with that of the two-to-four stage—"

The toilet flushed, distracting Diana a second time. She looked up to see Alex coming out of the bathroom wiping his lips. He was definitely pale as he staggered back to his desk.

"Can I get you anything?" asked the loyal Alice.

Alex Hesse shook his head. "I'm fine," he said weakly.

"He's fine!" announced Alice to the world in general.

"Let's get to work," said Diana, and her lab assistants went dutifully off to their stations.

Larry Arbogast strolled into the laboratory. "Morning, everybody," he announced expansively. "Big Al, how they swingin'?" He stopped by the chimpanzee cage and gazed in for a minute at the newborn apelet and her ecstatic parents. Larry grinned. "Hey, she got her mother's lips."

Alex crooked a surreptitious finger at his partner, beckoning him into his corner. "What's up?" Larry asked under his breath.

Alex pointed to a window on his computer monitor. "My HCG levels aren't where they should be," he said quietly.

Larry Arbogast peered at the screen. "Yeah, I see," he agreed. "We'll up the hormone supplements five milliliters. How're you feeling?"

Alex shrugged. "I still can't keep anything down."

"Morning sickness," Larry said casually. "It'll pass. Eat some crackers."

Alex rubbed furtively at his chest. "And my nipples are very sensitive," he said in a low voice.

"What?"

"My nipples." Alex spoke a little louder. "Tingling."

"Tingling like sore, or like itchy?" asked Larry.

Arthur, Diana's lab assistant, who was working nearby, overheard their conversation and leaned over helpfully. "Do you surf?"

"What?" Alex had no idea what he was talking about.

"Surf, you know, surfing. I get that sometimes from paddling out. Something about the wax on the board and the salt water irritates them."

"Get what?" Jenny, the other lab assistant, wanted to know what they were talking about. "What do you get?"

"His nipples are tingling," supplied Arthur.

"I don't surf," Alex said.

"Could be your laundry detergent," Jenny offered in a confidential tone. "I used to get that when I used nonbiodegradable soaps."

Alex shook his head. "I don't think so."

Diana looked over, a little annoyed to see her assistants wasting precious lab time in chewing the fat with Dr. Hesse. After all, they were here to work. The university was underwriting serious scientific research, not a housewives' kaffeeklatsch.

Alex pulled Larry aside, where nobody could overhear them. "I don't know how much more of this I can take," he said, anguished.

Larry took an assessing look at his partner. It was true: Alex *did* look like shit. He was a pale yellow-green in complexion, and there were black circles around his eyes, making him look a little like a huge raccoon, maybe a panda bear. But he was by no means in bad shape. This was normal in pregnancy, nothing to get excited about. By the end of the trimester, Alex would be a great deal sicker. Not that there was any reason to mention that to him.

"Hey, you're doing great," Larry told Alex with hearty encouragement. "I talked to my guy at Lyndon this morning. They've seen the initial data and they're *very* excited. I'm meeting with their CEO at the convention in San Francisco next month."

Suddenly Alex groaned loudly and doubled over, clutching at his middle.

"Cramps?" Larry asked solicitously.

Too pained to talk, Alex could only grimace and nod wordlessly.

"Get some air, walk it off." Larry helped him to the lab door, looking for all the world like a small tugboat escorting the *QEII* out of harbor.

The two men walked out of the building together, Larry strolling nonchalantly and Alex huffing along, taking sharp, panting breaths. "I don't want to cut back the hormones and jeopardize the protocol," said Larry. "A little tingle and a tummyache isn't going to kill you."

"Dr. Hesse? Dr. Arbogast?" A clipped British voice called behind them.

Larry rolled his eyes heavenward. "Just what we need," he muttered.

Diana Reddin came trotting after them, looking purposeful. A Rollerblader was swooping down at thirty miles an hour in her direction, and she swerved to avoid him, but of course she swerved right into his path, and the skater went flying. Totally oblivious, Diana trotted on, catching up with Larry and Alex. "I don't mean to pry," she began, "I know this is none of my business, but—"

"What?!" Larry's paranoia was immediately triggered.

Diana looked uncomfortable and nibbled at her lip in that characteristic gesture of hers. She waved one hand in

the air in a circular gesture. "Well, I can't help notice—
the nausea, the lethargy, those empty little vials in the
bathroom wastebasket—" Diana broke off, hesitating to
continue. She was afraid of giving offense; on the other
hand, her intentions were good, she wanted only to help.

"Yes?" Alex looked at her anxiously. He knew what all
those symptoms added up to, and Diana, too, was an
expert in the field of reproduction. Could she possibly
have taken a wild guess and stumbled on the correct
answer? If there was one thing Diana was good at, it was
stumbling.

She came right out with it. "Do you have a substance
abuse problem?"

Alex exploded. "No! Absolutely not!"

"It's nothing to be ashamed of, you know," Diana said
gently. "Might even be hereditary. I was involved in an
Oxford study where—"

Alex suddenly clutched at his belly and uttered loud
moans, his knees began to buckle, and he leaned against
Larry for support.

"Doctor! Are you all right?" Diana's lovely face was
the picture of concern.

"Just a little . . . It'll pass," Alex said weakly. He
was finding it very difficult to stand, so he laid himself
down on the lawn. Larry bent over him, and Diana knelt
down close beside him.

"Worse?" asked Larry.

"The cramps again . . . It's bad," Alex gasped.

"What's wrong with him?" Diana asked.

Larry shook his head in resignation. "I . . . I guess
we should tell you about his condition," he said slowly.

Alex looked very alarmed. "We should?" Larry shot

him a significant look, a look that said plainly, *Just leave it to me and follow my lead.*

"Can you keep a secret?" Larry asked Diana.

"Well, sure."

"He's been testing a formula, on himself. That's the little bottles. The nausea, the tingling nipples, those are the side effects, I'm afraid." He lowered his voice. "Just between us, right?" he urged in a guarded tone.

"Of course," Diana assured him. She glanced at Alex, who was still clutching at his belly and looked agonized.

Larry waxed lyrical, as only he knew how. "There is a tragic disease that afflicts the men of his village in Austria. They even named it after the place. Gelandesprung Syndrome. You've heard of it?"

"No," said Diana.

Alex opened his mouth to protest. *Gelandesprung?* What kind of idiotic fabrication was that? Alex Hesse was born and raised in Vienna. But he didn't dare to interrupt Larry, who was on some kind of roll!

"I'm not surprised. It is endemic only to a few places in all the world."

"What is it?" Diana's scientific curiosity was aroused. A new disease, one that she had never heard of, was intriguing to her.

Larry thought furiously, but nothing came immediately to mind. He was running out of inventiveness. "It is . . . a terrible, relentless . . . debilitating . . ."

"Fatness," put in Alex, who had just noticed an extremely large woman walking by.

"Yes." Larry picked up on it at once and was back on his roll without missing a beat. "Fatness striking young men in their prime, turning them into big, wheezing . . ."

"Strudelhunds," supplied Alex.

"Strudelhunds?" echoed Diana.

"Pastry hounds," Alex translated. "It is the insult they hurl at us." A fresh wave of cramps gripped him, and he groaned again, gripping his middle and gritting his teeth.

Before Larry could continue, he caught sight of Noah Banes walking in their direction. The head of the science department was reading through a scientific paper as he walked, and had not yet noticed Alex, who was not supposed to be anywhere near the Lufkin Center. For all Banes knew, Dr. Alexander Hesse had not only left the building, he had left the country. Larry caught Alex's eye and nodded in Banes's direction. Leave it to him. He would head Banes off.

"I'll get you some crackers or something," he told Alex. "Be right back." To Diana he said, "He'll be all right."

"Okay." She was not unwilling to accept the responsibility of looking after Dr. Hesse for a little while.

"Thank you, Larry," Alex said feebly, and watched his partner hurry off.

Dr. Diana Reddin was still puzzling over Gelandesprung Syndrome. "But you, you're not fat—"

"Only because of the formula," Alex put in quickly. "I have only . . . ," he did some quick mental calculations, ". . . nine more weeks of the protocol. I have been synthesizing the drug in the lab. Soon, I will send the results to Vienna, where they will review it and, hopefully, approve its use and finally end the suffering of my *landesmanner.*" Alex was secretly astonished at his own newfound glibness and his strange ability to improvise lies. He'd been spending far, far too much time with Larry Arbogast, he decided.

Meanwhile, Larry had "accidentally" bumped into Noah Banes. "Banes! Just the man I wanted to see!"

From his great height, Banes looked down his haughty nose at the small man before him. "Whatever for?" he asked coldly. As far as Banes was concerned, Dr. Arbogast and Dr. Hesse were history, a failed experiment to be swept up and disposed of with the daily trash.

"Well, to say hi! It's funny how you don't appreciate someone until they're gone," Larry said smoothly.

"I'm still here. It's *you* that's gone." Banes regarded the little man with suspicious eyes. "What are you up to, Arbogast?"

"I have a couple of questions about our contract. You got two minutes?" With his hand in the small of Banes's back, Larry steered the department head off in another direction.

Alex remained on the grass with Diana. He was feeling really unwell, but he was rather glad of her company. She was a strikingly attractive woman whose slenderness appeared to advantage in her silk blouse and a skirt that revealed the length of her legs. Her eyes, he noticed again, were a really startling shade of blue.

A few feet away, a number of people were staring at them. They must present a strange sight, the two scientists in the grass, one kneeling, the other doubled over wincing. "I'm so humiliated," Alex mumbled, pained.

"Don't be," Diana said gently, wiping his sweaty forehead to comfort him. "People get sick. Nothing humiliating about it."

"I feel as though I've lost control over my body," said Alex sadly.

"Control's important to you, isn't it?" asked Diana.

"What do you mean?"

Diana tried to keep her voice and expression casual. "Oh, the same three shirts, week in, week out. The liverwurst and apple, every day, precisely at noon. The little ritual with the crossword puzzle—"

"I like order." Alex cut her off, irritated. "What's wrong with that?" he demanded defensively.

"Nothing." She shrugged. "It's just an observation."

"And I *don't* like being sick. Is there something wrong with *that*?"

"No, no," Diana said hastily; she had not intended to offend Dr. Hesse. Sometimes she was so awkward she could just kick herself. It was her lack of easy sociability that accounted for it. Now she tucked her elegant foot even more firmly into her red-lipped mouth. "It's just that men are— Oh, never mind."

"Men are *what*?"

Diana took a deep breath. "Well, they're so *pathetic* when it comes to pain. A little discomfort and you turn into absolute *babies*! Try being a woman some time. Your body goes peculiar with your first period and doesn't quit until menopause. A lifetime of leaking and swelling, spotting and smears, raging hormones, crippling cramps, yeasts. And that's if everything's *normal*."

Alex was taken aback by this sudden emotional overflow from the usually reticent Dr. Reddin. He didn't know what to answer. "I've never wanted to be a woman," he said quietly.

Diana nodded, a little embarrassed by her own outburst. Then she smiled, and her entire face lit up and looked beautiful. "I'm just saying . . ." she said apologetically.

Suddenly, both of them realized at the same time that Diana was still stroking Alex's forehead, by now rather vigorously. Even used vigorously, her competent hands were soft and gentle, a woman's hands. Self-consciously, she removed her hand, and Alex immediately felt a small—ever so small, yet sharp—pang of loss.

He suddenly realized that they had never been alone together before. In fact, they had never even spoken to each other without a couple of lab assistants hovering within earshot. As an experience, sitting here on the grass with her was, as Alex would say, not unpleasant. No, not unpleasant at all.

It would have been astonishing indeed if neither of them had had even a fleeting remembrance of that first, gratefully impulsive kiss that Diana had planted on Alex when he'd saved her and her precious eggs from crashing into a wall. The thought was in the mind of each of them. Alex could actually feel Diana's lips on his own.

But this was no time to become interested in a woman, no matter how like-minded, how sweet, intelligent, or attractive, no matter how shapely her legs, how curved her white neck, how soft or gentle her hands. For one thing, there was the protocol to consider. He had to put his scientific research first. For another, he'd just been telling her the biggest pack of lies he'd ever uttered in his life. Gelandesprung Syndrome. *Gott in Himmel*, what next?

Chapter Four

Great Expectations

"Perfectly normal, not to worry," Larry Arbogast told his nervous patient over the telephone when she called to tell him that she was showing a little blood. He held the phone cradled under his bottom chin as he mixed a martini with his free hands. "Just stay off your feet, use an ice pack for a few minutes every hour, and call me in the morning." As he hung up the phone, Alex came into the kitchen wearing sweats and zipping up his hooded sweatshirt.

"How ya doin', Mama?" Larry grinned. He took a long, refreshing sip of his martini.

"I'm going to miss the ten o'clock evaluations tonight," Alex replied, ignoring the jest. "We can extrapolate variances with the morning readings."

"Where are you going?" Larry looked concerned.

"I am unfit," said Alex.

"Unfit? Unfit for what?"

"I understand that there are to be negative side effects in this protocol, but I see no reason why I shouldn't combat them with an increase of good conditioning. I am therefore going to the gym for a long session of exercise."

"Whoa, wait just a minute." Larry felt a chill of apprehension. "Are you sure that's such a good idea? You can't put physical strains like that on a new pregnancy," he cried.

"It's an excellent idea. Don't worry," Alex answered seriously. "I don't intend to do any heavy lifting, stretching, or squatting. I want to work on my upper body strength and my calf muscles. I shall use the machines and the cinder track. And I plan to swim a few laps, just a light regimen. But if I don't get some decent exercise, my continued good health might well be negatively impacted, and I'll be *very unhappy*. Do you understand me?" Alex bent a stern brow at Larry, who quailed under it.

"Larry? *Larry!*" a voice hollered from the living room. An all-too-familiar female voice. Larry Arbogast made a face and headed for the living room.

"Angela, what the hell are you doing here?" Angela Arbogast was fiddling with the throw pillows from the couch, a grim look on her face.

"Leave those alone, Angela!" How could a woman so small and so cute be such a giant-sized pain?

"Don't snap at me!"

"It's *my* house now," Larry pointed out.

"The decor of which is part of my legacy and a reflection on me." Angela rearranged the throw pillows to her satisfaction. "Floral, houndstooth, *then* paisley."

"What do you want?" sighed Larry. He felt beset on all sides, and he wished with all his heart that the damn protocol was over, and that he was already living high off the proceeds. He was counting the days. Oh, well, only another couple of weeks and then out.

At that moment, Alex Hesse came through the living room on his way to the front door. He was carrying a gym bag. Larry made the introductions. "Alex, Angela. Angela, Alex. Colleague of mine."

Alex yawned, then belched. The development of the fetus was starting to put pressure on his gut, and he was almost always dyspeptic these days. "Excuse me. Hello."

"Charmed," said Angela sarcastically. Larry and his "colleagues." What a bunch of losers! But she was curious to know what this Alex was doing here, coming and going as if he owned the place.

Alex headed for the door. Larry looked after him, anxious. He hated the idea of Alex taking rigorous exercise. Why couldn't he just be content to lie around the house for three months, blimping up, gobbling ice cream and chocolate donuts? "Just take it easy, okay?"

Alex grunted. "Tonight I will feel like myself again." He closed the door behind him. Angela raised a puzzled eyebrow at Larry.

"He's going through a confusing time," Larry explained. "I'm letting him stay here with me for a few weeks. Now, what are *you* doing here?"

"I don't like Sneller," Angela said firmly. "I want you to be my doctor."

Larry sighed. "Angela, we've been all through this. Ned Sneller's a top, top guy."

"I'm *not* going back to him," Angela said with finality.

Larry threw his hands up in exasperation. "I can't deal with this! Where's the goddamn father?"

Angela's huge eyes clouded, and she looked away uncomfortably. "I haven't been able to reach him," she admitted finally.

"What? He's disappeared?"

Angela shrugged. "They're touring Europe or Asia, I forget which."

"*Who* is?"

"Aerosmith."

Her reply stunned Larry, absolutely floored him. "One of Aerosmith knocked you up?" he gasped. His mind reeled. His own ex-wife, a forty-one-year-old woman, had turned into a groupie for a rock-and-roll band?

"What a *lovely* phrase," snarled Angela, and their conversation began to escalate into a fight, as used to happen in the final months of their marriage.

"*Excuse* me," Larry snarled back, "but I'm a little shocked here, okay?"

"Well, deal with it!" Angela's round chin came up defiantly.

"I don't *have* to deal with it! We're divorced!"

For the first time, Angela noticed Larry's left-hand ring finger. "You're still wearing your wedding ring," she remarked, surprised.

"What?"

"The ring," she pointed. "How come?"

Caught off guard, Larry didn't have a glib excuse ready. "It's . . . uh . . . stuck," he lied. "Tried everything." He shrugged sheepishly.

Angela nodded. She knew her ex-husband well, and could tell when he was lying. Tried everything, right? Tried everything except taking it off. Unconsciously, she touched her bare ring finger. She'd taken her own ring off as soon as she'd filed for divorce. "I'm not going back to Ned," she said again, and it was plain that she meant it.

Larry knew when he was beaten. "Okay," he sighed. "Call Louise in the morning. She'll fit you in."

A small smile tugged at the corners of Angela's full

lips, but she repressed it. "Okay. Thank you." Having gotten what she'd come for, she headed for the door.

"Angela?"

Almost out the door, she turned back. Larry was regarding her with a strange expression on his face. "I *am* happy for you," he said quietly.

Larry's gentle words took her totally by surprise. Angela looked at him sharply to see if he was making fun of her, but he appeared to be entirely sincere. This time Angela couldn't repress the smile, but she kept it brief. She felt a sort of melting start up inside her, and she recognized the feeling. So she got a grip on herself and hustled out of there on the double, before the gooey feeling could spread to other parts of her body.

Alex Hesse wasn't doing too well. He felt puffy and bloated and was further out of condition than he'd thought. He had to leave the Nordic machine in a hurry three times to go and pee, and once in an even greater hurry to throw up. When he ran his laps on the cinder track, he became so sleepy he nearly fell over his own feet. And, worst of all, the second he dived into the Olympic-sized gymnasium swimming pool, he couldn't help his bladder's reaction; Alex peed in the water.

This was complete and utter humiliation. Alexander Hesse had never in his life urinated into a swimming pool. He dragged himself out of the pool, showered off, checked out, and climbed into his Jeep. The entire evening at the gym had been a fiasco. He was pregnant, and that was that. Don't fight it. Only a few more weeks and then it would all be over. Then the first thing he would do was get back into shape, he promised himself.

A very strict regimen of body sculpting and weight training. Alex wanted his figure back.

Meanwhile, as he was driving home to Larry Arbogast's house, a sudden desire for mint chocolate chip ice cream overcame Alex, and he stopped the Jeep outside an ice cream store close by Ghiradelli Square. He *had* intended to buy only a cone, but he came out of the store with a full quart.

The weeks passed quickly, until at last eleven of the twelve weeks of the trimester were gone. Alex took to sleeping most of the day, working in the lab in the evenings, and living mainly on mint chocolate chip ice cream, which he was consuming at the rate of a half gallon at a time.

Larry still tested Alex every day, entering the results into his notebook computer, results that Alex would turn into impressive data—charts and graphics and printouts—on his computer in the corner of Diana's lab. So far, so good. The fetus was developing nicely, getting its nutrition through its placenta from the lining of its home in Alex Hesse's peritoneal cavity. Expectane, supplemented by the female hormones, seemed to be doing the trick.

Larry ran the ultrasound device over the gel on Alex's bare belly and studied the blurry images on the monitor. Alex lay quietly on Angela's flowery bed, his shirt off, his attention focused on the television set on the dresser. A commercial was on the screen, and Alex watched it intently.

Shown was a softly lit scene in a hospital room. A new father, still dressed in the delivery-room scrub suit, was sitting on his pretty young wife's bed. She was holding their crying newborn baby in her arms as her husband spoke into the bedside telephone.

"Dad? I know we haven't talked in a while, but . . . I thought you might like to say hello to your granddaughter." The young man sounded tentative, a little shy, but eager for his dad's approval.

There was a quick cut to a craggy-faced curmudgeon Dad, sitting in his living room, listening with gratification and smiling into his end of the telephone. The music swelled up and over, and then a voice-over said, "Fleet Long Distance. The lines of communication."

Alex sniffled, and a tear glistened in his eye. He wiped it away with one finger.

"You okay?" asked Larry.

"He wasn't going to call his father, but then he did," and Alex sniffled again.

Larry shot him a very dubious look. What the hell was wrong with the big dweeb? "Get a grip!" he advised, and turned to his notebook computer, into which he typed some data.

"I don't know how much longer I can stand this!" Alex cried, anguished.

"Courage, big guy. It's just another week. Everything's right on track."

"I'm sorry," Alex said softly. "I'm not myself."

Larry shut off the computer and the ultrasound and pulled his jacket on. "I'll be back late tonight; don't wait up," he said casually.

"Why? Where are you going?" A look of alarm appeared on Alex's large face. He trailed Larry from the bedroom, through the living room, and to the front door of the house.

"The pharmaceuticals convention at the Hyatt. I'm meeting the Lyndon guys."

"Take me with you," said Alex unexpectedly.

"Nah, you stay here, take it easy—"

"*Please!*" Alex threw himself against the front door, blocking it. "I'm pregnant and all alone."

Alarmed, Larry reached up and grabbed his partner firmly by the shoulders. "Alex! You're not *pregnant,* okay? Think of it like you swallowed a piece of gum. Little piece. Dentyne."

"I won't be in the way," begged Alex. His eyes filled with tears, and his lashes fluttered unhappily. "Please. I'm feeling so isolated."

Larry let his breath out in a whoosh. "All right, all right. Just don't do that thing with your eyes." He went out to his car while Alex ran to get his shirt, tie, and jacket.

It was a good party, an expensive party, sponsored by a pharmaceuticals company with very deep pockets. The vintage wine was flowing free, the munchies were delicious, and the jazz combo and band singer were making sweet sounds together. Like a small, chubby, heat-seeking missile, Larry had quickly located his targets—four executives from Lyndon Pharmaceuticals wearing "Hello, My Name Is" labels pasted to their dark suits. He was well into his Expectane spiel, with Alex nowhere in sight, thank God.

"In the United States alone, we'd be looking at five million prescriptions a year, *easy.*" There was a murmur of approval from the pharmaceuticals executives.

"What's your window on these human experiment results?" asked one of the Lyndon people.

Larry lowered his voice confidentially. "Just between us? We'll have initial results in a couple of weeks."

Another gratifying murmur; they were evidently impressed. Conspiratorial handshakes all around. "We're *very* interested. Keep us posted."

"Will do," said Larry with a grin, and under his breath he added "Yesss!" But the grin faded from his face when he turned and saw Noah Banes standing just behind him, eyeing him as he sipped his drink. How much had the oversized Pez head overheard? Had he heard the Lyndon executive speak those damning words "human experiment results"?

"B-Banes," stammered Larry. "What are you doing here?"

Banes smiled his ophidian smile, and his dark eyes glittered. "You know me, Larry, always with my ear to the ground. Interesting little pitch with the Lyndon folks. As you know, human experiments would be outside of university and FDA guidelines."

So he *had* heard. *Careful, Larry,* he told himself. "I'm just trying to raise a little awareness and some new funding," he said as smoothly as he could manage. "So I'm letting people think it's further along than it is."

Noah Banes uttered a harsh laugh. Something was going on here, that was for sure, and he didn't trust Dr. Lawrence Arbogast any farther than he could kick him. "Oh, come on, Larry! As my old ma used to say, 'I may have been born yesterday, but I stayed up late studying.' *Is* there a woman out there, taking Expectane?"

"Absolutely not," Larry answered with great sincerity and, as it happened, with perfect truth.

"Larry! Noah! Hi!" Alex Hesse waved from across the room and came weaving his way through the crowd toward them, a blissful grin on his face. He breezed up to the two men, his eyes shining brightly.

"Alex? Where've you been?" Larry demanded.

The grin on the big man's face broadened. "I had a walk, and then a wonderful massage in the health club and then took a nap right there on the table." A waiter was passing them with a tray of canapés, and Alex snared him. "Franks in blankets! My favorites!" he enthused, snagging about a dozen hors d'oeuvres and piling them on a napkin.

Noah Banes's eyes narrowed, and he looked at Alex very closely. There was something not quite . . . He wasn't sure what . . . but he was puzzled. Alex was definitely not acting like himself. He didn't look like himself, either.

"Alex, you're looking . . . what's the word . . . *radiant!*"

Radiant. A well-known buzzword applied to pregnant women since the dawn of time. "We really should be going," Larry said quickly. *Before this moax puts two and two together and comes up with pregnant.*

"Yoo-hoo!" caroled a woman's voice. "There you are!" Diana Reddin was about ten feet away, bobbing up and down in the crowd of party-goers and waving violently at them. She was looking very fetching in something clinging and cut low that showed off her lovely shoulders and long swan's neck. She started over to them, straight into the path of a waiter carrying a full tray of drinks. The tray went flying, coming down with a splintering crash, but Diana didn't even notice.

Alex, Larry, and Banes winced. "It's a wonder that woman's still alive," muttered Larry.

"She looks very beautiful tonight, don't you think?" Alex murmured.

"Diana, darling, where have you *been*?" gushed Banes. He reached out one long arm, intending to wind it around Diana's waist in a show of affection, but she evaded him nimbly.

"Long line for the loo. Hello, hello." She smiled at Larry and Alex.

Alex held out his loaded napkin. "Hors d'oeuvre?" he offered.

Diana took a pastry-wrapped frankfurter and bit into it happily with her strong white teeth. "Sausage rolls! I love these!"

"They're my favorite." Alex grinned.

Diana Reddin craned her head back to stare up at him. There was a positive glow emanating from Alex Hesse. It was very attractive. "You look so . . . enthusiastic . . . tonight," she remarked approvingly.

"Yes," added Noah Banes, probing. "I've never seen you quite so lit up. So what's the good news?"

"Life!" cried Alex buoyantly, waving his arms. "Music and friends and franks in blankets and—"

Larry grabbed a tight hold on one of the big dweeb's waving arms. "We really should be going."

Alex pulled his arm away easily and leaned closer to Diana, speaking to her in an intimate manner. "Going, going, always going. Then one day—gone."

"Poof. Just like that," Diana agreed. The two of them exchanged goofy smiles.

"When we should be pausing to hear the joyful melody of life itself," Alex philosophized. Larry stared at him as though he were crazy; Noah Banes looked puzzled, but Diana Reddin found herself being curiously drawn to him. She moved a few steps closer to Alex.

"Exactly," she said.

"He doesn't get out much," Larry said apologetically to Banes, to cover for Alex's bizarre behavior.

The music was swelling now, into the old standard song "I've Got You Under My Skin." Alex hummed a few bars. "I've always loved this song," he told Diana. "Would you like to dance?"

Diana Reddin's face got that Bambi-caught-in-the-headlights look. "What?" she asked in a very small voice.

"Dance . . . to the music," Alex explained.

"Oh, *that.* I can't."

Banes edged closer, close enough to sniff the shampoo in Diana's soft hair. "With my lead, you'll feel like you've danced all your life," he purred urbanely. He had been trying to put the moves on Dr. Diana Reddin for weeks now, with a notable lack of success.

Looking crushed, Alex took a step backward, as he yielded to Banes. "Actually, I've never danced before in my life," he admitted gloomily.

That was all Diana had to hear. She couldn't dance and he couldn't dance; to her the solution was not only logical, it was inevitable. "Then let's do it!" she exclaimed, and taking the napkin full of franks from Alex, she handed it to a disconcerted Noah Banes.

Alex led Diana to the dance floor, deftly stepping on the long piece of toilet paper trailing from her heel and shaking it off his own shoe. What a gentleman! Then he took her hands and started to dance with her—after a fashion. They turned slowly around the floor like a couple of children in a ring-around-a-rosy game, having a wonderful time until Diana's heel broke right off her shoe.

She decided to ignore it, in order to preserve the sweetness of the moment, but Alex couldn't help noticing that she was starting to list badly to starboard. He looked down and saw that she was dancing—after a fashion—on only one heel. Immediately he kicked off one of his own shoes to compensate, and the two of them went lurching around the dance floor with serious faces, absorbed in the dance, oblivious to the rhythm of the music and to the fact that they were crashing into other dancing couples and that Diana had had another near miss with a busyboy carrying a tray of empty glasses. They were caught up in each other completely.

"You're really quite graceful for such a big man," Diana said sincerely.

Alex smiled down at her, and she smiled back up at him. They were both quite beautiful when they smiled. The moment and the music and their proximity to each other had them wrapped in a soft misty net of pleasure and even surprise. This was something that neither one of them had expected, this softness between them, this feeling of dawning wonder.

The song ended, but they continued to hold each other. Were they aware that there wasn't any more music? No, they were aware only of the meeting of their eyes and the touch of their hands, hers on his shoulder, his on her waist. It had happened; they had met cute, they had slowly and imperceptibly been drawn to each other; now they were both smitten, pretty girl and pregnant boy.

How long they would have gone on standing like this, blue eyes looking into blue eyes—well, who can tell? Diana and Alex were simply too happy to move, and they might be standing there yet except that Larry Arbogast reached up and tapped Alex on the shoulder with Alex's cast-off shoe.

"Okay, Cinderella. It's time to leave. *Seriously.*"

A flustered Diana took a step away from Alex. The mood shattered into a thousand pieces. "Yes, okay," Alex said reluctantly. He made a sort of bow to his partner, sweetly courteous. "Good night."

"Good night," Diana said softly. I really enjoyed that."

Before Alex could reply that he, too, had enjoyed their dance, Larry grabbed him and pulled him away with an astonishing show of strength born of a desperate need to get the hell out of there.

They had to wait at the Hyatt's valet stand for Larry's Chrysler to be brought around. It was raining, but while Larry chafed impatiently, Alex didn't seem to mind the rain. He was still thinking of the dance with Diana, and under his breath he kept humming "I've Got You Under My Skin," the song they'd been dancing to—after a fashion. He kept rubbing at his cheek with the back of one hand.

"Feel how soft my skin is." Alex offered his cheek to Larry.

"It's time. I want to close out the experiment," Larry said firmly. He'd been thinking about this a lot in the last few minutes. "Banes is sniffing around, and your hormone surges are getting out of control."

"But there's still a week until the trimester's over—" began Alex in protest.

Larry shook his head. "We have enough data already, and the Lyndon guys are *poised.* I don't want to risk taking it any further."

Alex said nothing, but he turned his face away, biting

at his lip while tears started up in his eyes. Larry tried to ignore his expression, but he couldn't. "What?!"

The big man sighed softly. "Sometimes, you know, I can't help but wonder what it would be like . . ."

The Chrysler pulled up. "What *what* would be like?" asked Larry.

"Having my baby," Alex said shyly.

"That's *it!*" Larry exploded, climbing into the driver's seat and banging the door shut. "We're closing out the experiment *now*! Tonight!"

Alex stepped into the passenger's seat and carefully buckled his seat belt. His lips were trembling with emotion, and he was very near tears. "I never realized how lonely I was."

Larry angrily turned the ignition key. "So buy a dog!" he snarled. The Chrysler leapt forward.

It was decided, then. Tonight Alex would terminate his so-called "pregnancy." It would be a simple matter, with no surgery involved. All it took was for Alex to put an end to his frequent doses of hormone-laced Expectane. So that was it. One trimester and out. Now that Alex didn't need daily monitoring, there was no longer any reason for him to be living over at Larry's house. It was time for Alex Hesse to go home and resume a normal life.

Alex was unexpectedly quiet as he packed his bags in the rose-strewn room that used to be Angela Arbogast's. Outside the windows, high winds and heavy rain rattled the glass panes, while lightning flashed and thunder boomed. But Alex Hesse was oblivious to the weather; his thoughts were very much somewhere else.

Alex was quiet as Larry drove him home, up and down

the dizzying hills of San Francisco, to his own apartment; he was quiet as they were buffeted by the blinding rain while unpacking his bags from the trunk of Larry's car. But as they rode up in the elevator with the suitcases, he said, "With Moe, I tapered off his dosage gradually, to aid his system in hormonal rebalancing."

Larry shook his head energetically. "You're not Moe. You go cold turkey. You may have a couple of rocky days, but I don't want to chance any complications. Just stop taking the Expectane, and the embryo will break down and be reabsorbed naturally into your body."

"And then, back to my old self," Alex said unenthusiastically.

"Yeah, your old self." Larry had forgotten Alex Hesse's old self—dour, humorless, not much fun to be around. "Won't that be great?"

They were carrying the luggage out of the elevator when Alex was hit by a sudden thought. "Does the egg's donor have any claims on the procedure?"

"No, none at all," Larry answered blandly.

"Where *did* you get it, by the way?" Alex asked suddenly, "The egg?"

Eleven weeks had passed without the question ever coming up, so by now Larry had been pretty sure he was home free. Now there it was, Alex asking about the egg, and Larry was going to have to lie his head off. He hesitated only a fraction of a second. "Uh . . . a colleague of mine. An anonymous harvest. He had a couple of spares."

Alex appeared to accept Larry's explanation without question. He inserted his key in the apartment door and threw it open. Before he could switch on the lights, the room was illuminated briefly by a jagged flash of lightning close to the windows. A split second later all went dark again. Alex turned on the overhead light, and both men came inside and dropped the bags.

"Home sweet home, huh?" Larry looked up at the big man, noticing that Alex really did look pretty lonely standing there by himself. He wasn't such a bad guy when you got to know him. Larry rubbed his hands together. "So. Hey. I'll get the data off to the guys at Lyndon, and I'll be in touch the moment I hear anything."

"Okay," said Alex without expression.

"Okay, then. Good work." Larry held his right hand out, and Alex shook it stiffly. Then, astonishingly given both their personalities, they hugged briefly, slapping each other on the back. If you had predicted three months ago that Dr. Lawrence Arbogast and Dr. Alexander Hesse would be hugging each other, they would have hauled you away in a rubber suit. But there they stood, one really big man and one really small man, with their arms wrapped around each other, patting each other awkwardly on the back. Go figure.

Embarrassed, they broke off the clinch and Larry turned to leave. But something made him turn back in the doorway and ask, "You okay?"

With a lump in his throat that made him unable to speak, Alex could only mutely nod his head yes, but it was an unconvincing sort of nod. He was still very downcast. Larry looked around the apartment. "You know," he said thoughtfully, really concerned about the big dweeb, "you really ought to think about that dog."

"I'm allergic," Alex said glumly.

Larry gave a too-bad shake of his head. Alex made the

effort and managed a rather dim smile and a thumbs-up gesture. Relieved, Larry returned it and left.

The pouring rain outside only increased Alex's feelings of depression and isolation. Sluggishly he unpacked and hung up his clothing; sluggishly he unpacked his toiletries and scrubbed his teeth; sluggishly he put on his pajamas and climbed into bed. The world seemed a very bleak and lonely place to him. Alex even missed Larry; he wasn't such a bad fellow when you got to know him, he thought.

Lying in his bed under the sheet, Alex took off his wristwatch and placed it on the bedside table. He reached over to turn off the night-light; he didn't feel like watching The Weather Channel tonight; he didn't even feel like a cup of cocoa. Suddenly the alarm on the watch went off. *Beep. Beep. Beep.* Startled, Alex looked at the time. The wristwatch alarm was his signal to gulp down another dose of Expectane, but of course as of tonight he wasn't going to be taking Expectane anymore. Cold turkey.

Beep. Beep. Beep. Alex found himself staring at the wristwatch. His feelings were in turmoil, conflicted, tearing him apart. His baby. Three months and out, that was what he'd agreed to. He couldn't decide. At last he stood up and walked slowly into his bathroom. The case of Expectane was sitting on the bathroom sink; he had been planning to flush the contents of the little bottles down the toilet, but somehow he hadn't. Alex opened the case. A few vials of Expectane were left, and he looked down at the little bottles with a grave face, as though they held his future, which they did,

Slowly, deliberately, he took one of the vials out of the case and held it up, looking at it for a long time, his brain

78

working furiously. He took out the stopper. I'll have to avoid Larry as much as possible, he thought.

"I don't know if you're a boy or a girl," he said softly, to himself, to the little creature growing inside him. "I'll call you . . . Junior."

Alex Hesse drank down the contents of the vial. He was making the deepest, most serious commitment he had ever made in his life. He was agreeing to bring another human being into the world, a helpless life for which he would be totally responsible. He agreed to love and cherish it, to be a parent to it, to introduce it to everything it would ever need in life. The very thought of it was terrifying. Oddly enough, not once did he think about making scientific history or joining the pantheon of the great.

Outside, there was a explosively loud boom of thunder and a bright flash of lightning. But Alex was suddenly, unaccountably, completely happy.

Chapter Five

Second Trimester

In the next ten weeks, Alex Hesse progressed into his second trimester. He was starting to go through some very heavy physical changes. The growing baby inside him was taking up more and more room, making increased demands on Alex's internal organs. It pushed uncomfortably against his bladder, his kidneys, his spleen, his gallbladder, colon, and pancreas. Alex felt fatigued all the time, and his back hurt constantly. His legs were giving him trouble; painful cramps gripped and twisted his calf muscles in the middle of the night and woke him up yelling. During the day, the varicose veins that had recently appeared in his thighs were swollen and aching. He lay on his sofa sometimes for hours, with one hot water bottle pressed to his belly, and another to his back.

His emotional state vacillated back and forth like the pendulum in a grandfather clock, playing havoc with his peace of mind, now raising him to ecstatic joy, now plunging him down into despairing depression. When he was up, he felt fertile, happily expectant, creative, necessary. He felt at one with nature and the universe. When he was down, he felt frightened and bloated.

Alex maintained a fairly low profile, keeping pretty much to himself except for the hours he spent at the keyboard of his computer in his corner of Diana's laboratory, or working with chemicals at a lab table, formulating a new supply of his Expectane dosages, which he potentiated with female hormones. When he wasn't in the lab, he spent most of his time holed up in his apartment, going out only occasionally, on quick forays to the ice cream store. He had switched from mint chocolate chip to butter brickle, and he had escalated his consumption. By now he was spending almost as much on ice cream as he was paying for rent.

At home, Alex left his telephone answering machine on at all times, and whenever Larry Arbogast phoned, he was forced to leave a message. The message was always pretty much the same one—"Hey, big guy, I'm a little worried about you. Give me a call." But Alex would never call back. Sometimes he sat and listened to Larry's voice on his message tape, and he felt a pang, as though he had lost a really good friend.

There were times when all Alex could think about was his future with Junior. What did fate have in store for them? Would he ever be able to tell his child the means by which he or she had come into the world? Would he ever find the right woman to share the child's parenting, and would he be able to share his secret with her? It was against Alex's nature to lie and dissemble and conceal, although he had been doing a lot of that in the past six months. He often wished he could open up to somebody sympathetic, to actually lean on another person's shoulder, maybe even shed a tear or two and get a hug. Alex badly needed a hug.

He enjoyed thinking about his baby. Often Alex would try to picture a future in which he watched Junior growing up, learning to walk and talk and think for him/herself. Would he/she be a good student, interested in science, a good athlete, to follow in his . . . father's . . . footsteps? Would they be good friends? He would need all his parenting skills, but what if they weren't enough? A feeling of panic gripped Alex, and he fought it down, concentrating on more mundane matters.

Would he/she need orthodontia? Alex himself had a large space between his two front teeth which had never bothered him, but he wanted his baby's smile to be perfect. He wanted everything to be perfect.

Alex imagined taking his offspring back to Austria, to show him/her off to his own parents. But what would he tell his *muttie*? That her grandchild Junior was adopted? What if the baby looked like him . . . although not, please God, exactly like him down to the last detail, as in that awful nightmare . . . how would he be able to explain the resemblance away with a story of adoption? Who would believe him?

What if Junior had his mother's eyes? To be his baby's mother, would he ever find a woman who had those identical eyes? Oddly enough, Alex kept coming back again and again to Diana Reddin's eyes. A child would be lucky to have clear, intelligent, beautiful eyes like Diana's, but what were the odds? Diana Reddin's eyes were unlike any he had ever seen.

As for his relations with Diana, things had not progressed much beyond everyday common courtesy. They shared a lab and Alex benefited from Diana's ordering the chemicals he needed on her own budget, but that was all. This was strictly because Alex was making himself deliberately unavailable, emotionally as well as physically. If Diana Reddin had reason to expect that Alex would be phoning her after their dance that evening two-and-a-half months ago, or that by now they would be going out together and perhaps have become involved in a deeper, more intimate relationship, she said nothing out loud to him or to anyone else, hiding her disappointment with ladylike class.

But Diana couldn't hide her emotions from herself. What she felt for Alex was more than a passing attraction. He seemed to her to incorporate just about everything she had despaired of ever finding in a man. He was entirely her intellectual equal, something Diana hadn't often encountered. He possessed the same fervor—amounting almost to obsession—for hard work and dedication to science that motivated her. Alex was driven by the same ambitions and dreams—to discover an amazing new benefit for humankind.

But Alex Hesse was also surprisingly sensitive for so obviously masculine a man. He had that gentle feminine side that women cherish in a man. And that tall, rocklike, muscular body, oh my! Just the thought of his broad chest and flat belly made Diana feel strangely warm. She was powerfully attracted to him in the basic physical sense. No, bottom line: she wanted him, bad.

But if it was not to be . . . well, there wasn't much Diana could do about it except just to be her usual self—sweet, generous, thoughtful, and just a bit scatty.

As for Alex, he recognized profoundly that Diana was a very special person, and that her intelligence combined with her occasional shy awkwardness made her different from anybody he'd met, giving her an irresistible appeal. He felt a startling connection—almost electric—with her that he had never felt before, and which went deeper than the merely professional bonds they shared, being research scientists.

But he was compelled to put his feelings on hold,

because the radical changes going on in Alex's body made it absolutely impossible for him to become involved with a woman now, much as his increased libido would enjoy it. From time to time, he would feel Diana's eyes on him in the laboratory, and when he looked up, he would find her staring wistfully at him. When she caught his glance, she would smile sheepishly and get back to her test tubes.

Alex promised himself that as soon as all of this was over and Junior was a reality, he would pursue his feelings for Diana. He would make it up to her. But for now he had to conceal his condition and his emotions as well.

As the weeks sped by, Alex's mood became one of withdrawn encapsulation. He had become totally self-absorbed, concentrated inside himself. Just as a placenta curves around a fetus, protecting it, nourishing it, so Alex Hesse's attention curved inward, around the new life growing inside him. Junior was *his* secret, his alone, a secret to keep and cherish.

Alex cried easily these days, even at foolishness like the Angel Soft commercial on TV, in which plump little babies floated heavenward on wings as soft as the advertiser's toilet paper. He listened to Mozart and Brahms so that the developing fetus would hear beautiful and soothing sounds. He found himself studying the glossy magazine photographs of adorable babies. He pored over mail-order catalogs of infant wear. He read a great deal, books with titles like *The First Miracle Year of Your Baby's Life, How to Parent Well,* and *Lucky You, You're Going to Have a Blessed Event*. He even read books about natural childbirth, although the only way that Junior could possibly enter the world was by c-section.

Physically Alex Hesse was going through heavy changes. The sleepiness of his early weeks began to dissipate, to be replaced by a kind of warm languor; his movements became slow and dreamy, as though he were walking on the floor of the ocean. He suffered from backache, headache, and flatulence, and he knew from his readings that what he had to look forward to in the months ahead was constipation, hemorrhoids, and severe heartburn. On top of more backache, headache, and flatulence.

And, boy, did he ever have to pee, every half hour on the half hour! The growing fetus pressed on his bladder mercilessly. In addition, Alex he was getting frequent hot flashes, when he would break out suddenly into unaccountable bouts of perspiration.

This day Alex was sitting, as usual, at the keyboard of his computer, sweating profusely, watching the projection of the human figure rotate on the monitor. The figure now showed a swollen belly in profile, and Alex was typing in the caption to run across the bottom of the screen—"Twenty-One Weeks Impregnation." Suddenly he heard the most ungodly noise and looked up to see Diana Reddin coming in through the lab doors, singing.

"Happy Birthday to you . . . ," warbled Diana. She was pushing a lab cart on which stood—or rather, drooped—a large birthday cake that might have been tall and beautiful, but wasn't. The cake was obviously a homemade affair, into which someone had poured a great deal of affection and not a great deal of culinary expertise. Even the birthday candles were lopsided, leaning against one another drunkenly and already dripping hot wax on the frosting.

Behind Diana and the lab cart marched a strange little

procession: Larry Arbogast; the lab assistants Alice, Jenny, and Arthur; and, stomping along on bow legs at the front of the parade, Minnie and Moe the chimpan- zees. All of them were singing the "Happy Birthday" song, including the chimps, although their tune was off-key and the lyrics came out a garbled "Eek, Urp. Chirr chirr chirr."

". . . Happy Birthday, dear Alex, Happy Birthday to you . . ." And they all broke into applause.

Alex was genuinely moved. What a touching gesture! Such good friends! He stood up to acknowledge the applause, but didn't get up all the way. He held himself in kind of a hunched crouch, and he was wearing sweatpants and a very loose sweatshirt intended to conceal his body from view. "How did you know?" he asked.

"I looked it up in your file," Diana said and beamed.

"And you baked the cake yourself," gushed Alex, although that much was obvious to anyone's eye.

Diana regarded the floppy mess of cake and icing rather ruefully. "The ingredients mutated a bit, I'm afraid," she said apologetically.

"Happy birthday, big guy!" Larry said expansively. "Where've you been hiding?"

"I've been . . . very busy," Alex said evasively. But he was almost happy to see Larry. Even though he had good reason to avoid him, the last ten weeks had been rather cheerless without him. Alex had frequently missed the little man's energy and ebullience. Could he be growing to like Larry Arbogast, or was it merely senti- mentality from the female hormones that was washing over him?

"What, you can't even return a phone call?"

Alex shrugged. "The days are very full," he said simply.

"Well, come on," Diana chortled. "Make a wish."

Alex wiped the beads of sweat off his brow, closed his eyes, and blew out all the candles. His unspoken wish concerned Junior, of course, and the continuation of Junior's well-being. "It looks delicious." He smiled at Diana.

Diana cast a concerned eye over Alex's damp brow and cheeks. "Alex, you're sweating like a racehorse," she exclaimed. "Are you all right?"

"It's hot in here—"

Larry Arbogast gave the big man a long once-over. "No, it's not. And why are you hunched over like that?" A terrible suspicion was beginning to dawn in his quick brain. He began to add two and two.

Alex tottered unsteadily on his feet. His face was flushed, and large beads of sweat kept forming on his brow and rolling down his face. "My . . . back's out," he lied. "It sure *feels* hot in here." He had to get some of these clothes off before he passed out.

"Too much birthday excitement, perhaps?" Diana offered helpfully.

But Alex didn't hear her; he was struggling to get his sweatshirt off, and his ears were muffled by the cloth. He pulled it over his head, but he got tangled up in it, and his T-shirt came along with it for the ride. Suddenly, exposed for all to see, was Alex's naked belly. It was taut and swollen and about the size of a basketball.

"Whoa!" laughed Jenny and Arthur.

"No cake for you," Alice tut-tutted.

"Oh, dear!" cried Diana.

"Oh, *shit*!" yelled Larry as two and two suddenly

made a great big four, and the horrible realization washed over him, confirming his worst-case-scenario suspicions. The big dweeb was still pregnant, he was *pregnant* pregnant.

Larry was boiling mad, and he grabbed Alex and dragged him out of the lab without even stopping to think that a man his size should hardly have been able to budge a man Alex's size. It was like the bumblebee that scientists tell us is too heavy to fly, but the bee doesn't know anything about the principles of aeronautics, so he flies anyway.

Larry practically threw Alex into the passenger seat of the Chrysler and then screeched away from the curb, driving hell-for-leather to The Fertility Center, where he intended to make a full examination of this grossly pregnant male. Alex, on the other hand, remained calm, and sat quietly in the front seat next to him, fiddling with the shoulder belt to find a more comfortable position for his belly.

"What the hell are you thinking of?!" Larry yelped furiously.

"I want my baby," insisted Alex with a stubborn lift of his chin.

He wants his baby. "This is *crazy*! You know that, man!" shrieked Larry.

"I know what my heart tells me, that this is meant to be," Alex said quite placidly.

"Meant to be? *Meant to be?*" Larry's face was close to purple in color, and a large vein throbbed in his forehead. "God only knows where the placenta's attached itself. You've put your vital organ functions in enormous jeopardy. You're wreaking havoc with your hormonal and nervous systems—"

"I don't care," Alex said defiantly, although his lower lip trembled a little. "I want my baby."

The Chrysler careened into Larry's designated parking space. Fuming, Larry slammed on the brakes, hard, and scrambled out of the car. Alex got out with quiet dignity and followed Larry as the small man marched rapidly toward his office.

"You think you're the first clown who figured, 'Hey, I'm bored, think I'll have a child'?" demanded Larry.

"I didn't say that!" Alex protested. "Why are you being so negative?"

Larry stopped in his tracks and glared up at Alex, his hands balled into fists and planted on his hips. "Hello? Anybody *home*? You're a *guy*, Alex! This is totally against the natural order!! Guys don't have babies! We leave that to the women! It's part of the beauty of *being* a guy! Didn't your father ever have this talk with you?!!"

Now it was Alex Hesse's turn to get mad. He glared back down at Larry. "Look, if you won't help me, just say so! I don't need a lecture!"

Larry tugged him toward the entrance of The Fertility Center. "The hell you don't!" he growled.

Alex dug in his heels and resisted being pulled, an act which effectively put a stop to the pulling. He made a last-ditch attempt to communicate to Larry Arbogast something of what he was feeling. "If you could feel for one *minute* the sense of absolute joy and connection that carrying your baby brings, you would understand."

Larry became aware suddenly that a number of people were stopping to stare at them, caught up in this public little drama and mesmerized by the strange conversation. He gritted his teeth. "*Listen* to you! Have you lost it *completely*?! Now, come on inside!" With a mighty surge of effort, Larry succeeded in pulling Alex inside the building. He marched him down the corridor toward his office, like a prisoner under guard.

As usual, Larry's obstetrics/gynecology office was busy, with a waiting room filled with expectant mothers in various stages of pregnancy. Louise was at her desk. She could hear Larry and Alex coming down the hall, and Alex was saying some incredible things.

"Look, if I carry this baby to term, it will be a miracle," he was avowing. "And I will love and nurture that miracle, with everything that is in me." What the hell?

Larry opened the door, and he and Alex came in to find a waiting room full of pregnant women and a receptionist all staring at them, aghast. Without missing a beat, Larry turned on his customary charm.

"Ladies, sorry to keep you waiting," he said smoothly. "We'll just be a few minutes."

"Dr. Arbogast?" said Louise. "Your wife . . . uh . . . ex-wife's inside. You're late for her appointment."

Damn. He'd forgotten all about Angela. "Great." He nodded. To Alex, he said, "Take a seat."

Alex Hesse sat down in a chair in the corner and spread his knees apart to get more comfortable, folding his hands over an obviously protruding belly. What the hell? The expectant mothers, puzzled and confused, looked to Larry for the answer.

Larry smiled confidentially at them. "Nothing to be afraid of," he said soothingly. "He thinks he's pregnant. It's quite a fascinating case, really. I'm working in conjunction with the University's Psychiatric Center."

One of the women whispered to the expectant mother on her right, "He even looks pregnant."

91

Larry overheard her. "Autosuggestive physiological reaction. Incredible, isn't it?" He smiled with phony fondness at Alex, the condescending smile a genius scientist might grant to a favorite experimental animal, a little white rat, perhaps. Then he vanished into his office, leaving a waiting room full of curious women all staring at Alex Hesse.

In the examining room, Angela was already on the table, dressed in a clinic gown and covered with a sheet, her feet up in the stirrups. She was by now quite visibly pregnant. When Larry came in, Angela glanced significantly at the expensive watch on her petite wrist.

"Nice to see you, Angela," Larry said briskly. He approached and gave her belly a quick rub. "You can go now."

"That's *it*?!" Angela's jaw dropped down, and her brows drew together indignantly. "That's all? That's the whole examination?"

Larry wriggled uncomfortably. "Something important's come up," he told her hastily, as he helped her off the table. "We're going to have to reschedule."

"*I'm* important, Larry!" Angela cried, hurt. Why was he giving her the bum's rush like this?

"Yes, you are. Very important. This is something . . . *urgent*." Larry handed his ex-wife her clothes and began to set up the table again for Alex's examination, disposing of Angela's gown and linens, laying out fresh ones. Usually his nurse did jobs like this, but Larry wasn't letting anybody else in here with Alex.

"Are you going to be in here while I get dressed?" demanded Angela.

"Angela!" As though he hadn't seen her naked thousands of times. As though they hadn't had sex together before, during, and after their marriage.

She made a small moue of concession. "So I'm a little conflicted. It's allowed." As Larry hurried out, Angela began to dress. She was feeling suddenly very depressed; what she didn't realize consciously was that subconsciously she had been looking forward to Larry's paying some attention to her, even if it were only professional attention, even if she had to keep her feet in stirrups to get it.

Outside in the waiting room, the other patients were sneaking surreptitious peeks at Alex Hesse, fascinated by this big man's "illness." Dr. Arbogast had humored him, and so would they. This was better than *General Hospital*, and more plausible than most soap opera plots.

One woman cleared her throat. "How far along?" she asked Alex pleasantly.

"Twenty-one weeks," answered Alex.

"Is it your first?"

"Yes." Alex smiled shyly.

Another mother-to-be leaned forward. "Have you thought about names?"

"Junior, if it's a boy . . . and Junior if it's a girl?" There was a question mark in Alex's voice; he had not told anybody the baby's name so far, and he could have used a little validation from the outside world along about now.

"*Junior's* nice."

Larry came from his office into the waiting room on the double. "Come on!" he said urgently to Alex.

Alex followed him in, pulled off his T-shirt, and lay down on the examining table while Larry got the ultrasound machine ready. As the device roamed over

Alex's swelling belly, Larry studied the fetus's image on the monitor.

"There's the feet, the legs . . . This can't be happening!" He marveled at what he saw.

"But it is," said the blissful Alex, smiling. He strained to get a look at the monitor, where he could see a blurry fishlike little creature afloat in its placenta. It was a breathtaking, uplifting sight, even if vague, and Alex felt a warm thrill of happiness coursing through him. It was his first glimpse of his baby, his Junior.

"The thing that looks like a string of pearls there, that's the spine," explained Larry. "And there's the head."

Alex peered at the monitor. Yes! He could see it—the head, a tiny little face. Junior's face. Something of the wonder he was feeling, the sense of awe, communicated itself to Larry Arbogast. He, too, found himself strangely moved and thrilled.

Larry turned a dial on the machine, and suddenly the amplified sound of rapid thumping filled the examining room with its rhythm.

"Heartbeat," said Larry.

Alex looked worried. "It's very *fast!*"

"Hundred forty beats per minute. Perfectly normal," Larry reassured him. Together they listened to the infant's heartbeat for a few seconds, then Larry turned off the ultrasound monitor and sat down on his wheeled examining stool, rubbing his aching temples, thinking hard. Alex sat up and pulled his shirt over to him.

"In fact, *everything's* perfectly normal," said Larry, troubled, "excepting of course the little matter of the mom also being the dad." He turned a grave face to Alex. "If this gets out, your life will be over, you know. You'll be a freak, and I'll lose my license."

Alex's expression was just as grave. "It's not going to get out. I know that this is unfair to you, and dangerous for us both. But I want my baby, and I need your help."

Larry Arbogast sat thinking for a minute. Facing him was potentially the greatest commitment of his life, at least since the day he married Angela. And look how *that* had turned out. He sighed deeply. "Okay. You're going to move back in with me. I want you off your feet as much as possible."

"But—"

"But nothing," Larry said vehemently. "You're in for a *lot* of sacrifices. Better get used to it."

Racing through Larry's mind was the thought that they were both standing on the threshold of a medical miracle. The next few months would be very rough going, but if they could pull this thing off and Larry Arbogast could deliver Alex's living baby by ceasarean section, the financial rewards would be tremendous. Not to mention that medical history, especially the fields of obstetrics and human reproduction, would never again be the same.

What was racing through Alex's mind was an intense feeling of relief. He wasn't alone anymore with his secret. He had a friend and a doctor, and in a few months, God willing and Expectane working, he would have his Junior. Larry was an excellent obstetrician; Alex had every confidence in him.

"Okay," Alex said and nodded, accepting Larry's commitment and making one of his own in return. With only those two little syllables, "O" and "kay," Dr. Alexander Hesse accepted Dr. Lawrence Arbogast as his obstetrician and coconspirator, and made an implicit promise to obey his advice and instructions in all matters pertaining to the pregnancy. He climbed down from the table and pulled on his T-shirt.

"How are you feeling?" Larry asked in his best professional voice. "Anything unusual?" He smacked his forehead with the heel of his hand. "Jesus, what am I saying?"

But Alex took the question literally, as he usually did. "I've noticed that the normal side effects of pregnancy are greatly amplified with the Expectane dosage I have required. The morning sickness, the mood swings, the sleepiness, the sexual appetite—"

"Whoa!" Larry put up one hand. "Sexual appetite?!"

Alex nodded gravely. "Yesterday, just scooping the middle out of a honeydew melon gave me a *steifen*."

Larry shut his eyes and whimpered softly. This was going to be even harder than he'd thought, playing nursemaid to an overgrown, overeating, oversexed pregnant male. Like trying to baby-sit Godzilla.

About a month later, the university director Noah Banes sat at his desk going over a sheaf of papers spread out in front of him. There was a dark scowl on his haughty face as he added up the figures on his calculator. When he finished, Banes tapped his pen against his teeth, thinking hard. Then, his lips pressed together grimly, he slammed down the pen and pushed an intercom button to signal his personal assistant Samantha to come into the inner office.

"Samantha, correct me if you dare, but didn't I close down the Expectane project six months ago?"

"Yes, sir," Samantha answered.

Banes waved a handful of the papers under her nose. "Then *why* would Reddin's account show continuing requisitions for Expectane components? Is she up to something with Arbogast and Hesse?"

"Uh . . . I don't know, sir."

Banes's eyes glittered dangerously. "Would it be terribly difficult to find out?" he asked softly, icily. Samantha nodded and left, closing the door quietly behind her.

Something very odd was going on in Dr. Reddin's laboratory, that much was crystal clear, thought Banes. Arbogast and Hesse were up to something, something the FDA obviously wasn't aware of and hadn't approved, something that might jeopardize the good standing and high reputation of the university, not to mention those of Noah Banes. He made up his mind. He would have to keep a very sharp eye on that pair, starting today. He hadn't figured out yet exactly where Dr. Diana Reddin figured into this equation, but he was damn well going to find out. Banes had never got to first base with her and had given up trying. Screw her.

He was likewise damned if he was going to let those two get away with anything illegal or unethical on university property, not to mention using the university budget. What they might be doing on their own time in their own space with their own money was their own business . . . unless . . .

Unless what Hesse and Arbogast were doing was going to result in big profits and enhanced reputation. Why not? Alex Hesse was, Banes granted, a brilliant and dedicated scientist, and Larry Arbogast was, Banes granted, very shrewd. If they should really be onto something, if they were secretly testing Expectane on some forbidden protocol and it should turn out all right, then Noah Banes wanted to make sure the university got its cut.

His ambitious soul was titillated by the thought that, as the senior science department administrator, he would bask in the reflected glory of any Nobel-worthy discoveries made on the premises. And there would no doubt be a decent pay raise and a promotion in it for him. Who could tell just how high Noah Banes might rise clinging to the coattails of Expectane?

So what it all boiled down to was this: find out what was going on and cut the university in on their action for a suitably big piece. If those two didn't want to play, then Banes would cut them off at the knees, blow the whistle on Alex Hesse and Larry Arbogast to the FDA, and watch them fry. Either way, it was high time he began snooping around. There's no point in being cast as the villain if you don't get to act like one from time to time.

Chapter Six

Banes

As Alex Hesse entered his third and final trimester, the days began to drag slowly. At Larry's insistence, Alex stayed in bed every day for hours, chafing at the inactivity, feeling lonesome, missing the work and the laboratory and Diana and the chimpanzees. In the hours he spent out of bed, he nested. He fussed around the house, he dusted, he polished, he scrubbed, he vacuumed. He read *Good Housekeeping* and *Family Circle* and *Ladies Home Journal*. He watched the soaps. He developed a real attachment to *As the World Turns,* which he watched with a box of tissues on his lap and a bag of Double Stuf Oreos within reach.

Alex was running the vacuum cleaner over Larry's living room carpet now, while he listened to Larry's excuses on the cordless phone.

"Yes, I understand . . . I'm just a little disappointed. It's the third time this week I've had to eat alone." He listened for a few seconds more, then he said, "Hurry home. Oh, and don't forget to pick up the box of Cap'n Crunch. The big box. Thanks. Bye, now." He shut off the phone.

The doorbell rang. Alex switched off the vacuum and opened the door. Dr. Diana Reddin was standing on the step, looking adorable, tall and supple in a silk blouse and dark skirt, her thick hair tousled by the San Francisco evening breezes, a bunch of papers in her hand. "Hello," she said shyly.

At the welcome sight of her, Alex felt a burst of warm joy race suddenly through his veins. "Diana!" he exclaimed, happily surprised. He'd just been thinking about her, wondering what she was doing and if she was thinking of him, and he was feeling very left out; now here she was, and just looking at her face made him feel a lot better right away.

"Yes, it's me." They stood staring at each other for an awkwardly long moment, and then Diana thrust the papers at Alex. "Someone at the lab gave me these papers for you."

"Thanks. Who?"

"Who?" Diana's face clouded, and she suddenly looked flustered. "It's a lie," she blurted. "I really just wanted to see you." Her cheeks flushed a dark red.

"Well, it's nice to see you, too," Alex said happily. "Please, come in." As she passed him on her way through the door, he smelled the perfume on Diana's shining hair. Surreptitiously, he checked his own hair and breath to make sure they'd pass the closeness test.

Diana looked around the living room, which was large and well furnished and, thanks to Alex, spotlessly clean. "It's very generous of Dr. Arbogast to take care of you like this. He must be a nice man . . . underneath it all."

"He tries," Alex said.

"How are you feeling?" She looked curiously at him, wondering how he was getting along with his mysterious Gelandesprung Syndrome. Not very well, it seemed. He had evidently put on some more weight around the tummy, and his waistline was disappearing. If things went on this way Alex Hesse would soon become one of the *strudelhunds* he had told her about. Still, his eyes were bright and his complexion was fresh. His skin looked so soft that Diana wondered whether Alex was using a special cream on it, and if he was, would he tell her the name of it?

"Good, thank you."

"You look . . . um . . ." She searched for the right word. "*Glowing.*"

Alex nodded. "Yes, I feel very . . . alive. Please, let's sit." He indicated the sofa, covered in another of Angela's favorite florals, and Diana sat down. As he sat down next to her, Alex maneuvered for another heady whiff of her sweetly scented hair. Underneath the odor of perfumed shampoo, he detected another sort of perfume. It was the smell of the antiseptic soap they used in the laboratory, and it made Alex instantly nostalgic.

"Do you believe in reincarnation, past lives, that sort of thing?" Diana asked suddenly.

"No."

She shook her head. "Neither do I. Can't be that."

"What?" asked Alex, a bit puzzled. He didn't seem to be following the conversation very well.

Diana looked earnestly at him. "I have this strong, recurring feeling that I know you."

"You do know me," Alex pointed out literally.

"Yes. No." Diana shook her head, frowning with the effort of putting her strange feelings into words. "It's more than that. Perhaps . . . earlier?"

She twisted her body in her ferocious concentration on the topic. The front of her blouse fell open a bit, and Alex caught a glimpse of the lacy top of her brassiere.

Hypnotized, he moved closer to Diana, his eyes fixed on the tempting swell of her breasts.

Where could they have met before, and when? The question was like a thorn in Diana Reddin's paw, and she continued to gnaw at it. "I was born in Jakarta," Diana said suddenly. "Raised in England from the age of five. Kent, summers in Cornwall . . . Are you looking at my chest?"

"I was born in Austria," Alex said quickly. "Gelande-sprung."

"Home of the *strudelhunds*," said Diana with a smile.

"Ah . . . yes." Alex remembered in the nick of time the lie he'd told Diana. He moved an inch or so closer to her, aroused by the smell of her hair and the bit of lace that was winking coyly at him from out the top of her blouse. She was a tantalizing woman, even though she seemed to be largely unaware of her own appeal.

"I've never been to Gelandesprung, so it couldn't be that." Diana continued laying out the itinerary of her life, still trying to track down where she and Alex might have met before. There was something about him that was deeply familiar to her in a kind of mystical way, an uncanny sort of kinship, and it was a feeling totally apart from the physical and mental attraction he held for her. "I visited Salzburg once. Delicious chocolates, lovely clocks. Or was that . . ."

She broke off, suddenly conscious that Alex Hesse was behaving very strangely. It seemed to Diana that he wasn't listening to a word she was saying.

"Mmmmmmmmm," commented Alex, pretending to follow the conversation while all the while his yearning body was sending him strong *Gimme-Gimme-Gimme—I want—I want—I want—I want* messages.

102

"Alex?"

"Hmmmmmm?" replied Alex, tantalized as hell by Diana's unconscious sexuality.

"You're *twitching*!"

"Yes," he confessed. He could hardly deny it.

"Why?"

Alex twitched harder, scissoring his legs open and closed. He was in utter turmoil. "Does my body disgust you?" he asked at last.

"No, not at *all*!" Diana said and smiled. "I like a little upholstery in a man."

"You do?" Alex relaxed a little, encouraged by her words.

She smiled again, brightly, and Alex thought, How beautiful she is when she smiles!

"I was madly in love with my cousin Trevor for years, and he was *quite* portly," Diana confided.

"Maybe it's . . . physical?" Alex suggested tentatively, his heart in his mouth.

"Physical?"

"This connection."

Diana nodded her head vigorously. "Oh, it's definitely physical. Out of the blue I'll have these sudden pangs of concern for your well-being. It's most peculiar—" She became aware suddenly that Alex was looking at her in a way that meant only one thing, and it wasn't concern for well-being. "Oh! Oh, you mean . . . sex!"

"Yes," said Alex in a strangled voice.

Diana looked thoughtful for a moment. "I hadn't considered that," she mused, "but—yes. Why, of course!" Her face brightened: problem solved; thorny question answered. "That's it!" She threw herself onto her back on the sofa, with one arm raised enticingly above her head, in body language that said clearly, *Kiss me.*

Irresistably drawn, Alex moved closer. "Yes?" he asked hopefully.

"Yes," said Diana invitingly.

"Yes," breathed Alex, and he lowered himself gently onto her body. Their lips met tentatively in a sweet, soft, exploratory kiss. Then Diana and Alex pulled apart from each other, looking deeply into each other's eyes. Whatever they saw there roused them to fever pitch. Hungrily Alex and Diana fell on each other, kissing, nibbling, touching, barely breathing with the passion they were finally able to express after months of repression.

So caught up in each other and their mutual excitement were they that, climbing all over each other, they actually tumbled over the back of the sofa, landing on the floor with a thump. But that didn't stop them; nothing could stop Alex and Diana. Bed, sofa, floor, whatever— any reasonably horizontal surface would do just fine.

They began to tear at each other's clothing, feverish to feel skin beneath their hands, delirious with the joy that they knew fulfillment would bring them. They had both waited so long for this moment, and now it was here at last, and they weren't going to let it get away from them.

There was a sudden noise at the front door. A key turned in the lock; the door opened. A woman's voice bawled out, "Hello? Larry? It's me. I've let myself in."

Angela.

On the floor behind the sofa, Alex and Diana pulled apart with a mental *pop* like a cork leaving a champagne bottle, and frantically began to rearrange their disheveled clothing.

"Hello," Alex said sheepishly, sticking his head up over the back of the couch.

Angela scowled, and her large round eyes studied him suspiciously. "You're still here? Where's Larry?"

"Out."

"Mind if I wait?"

"Well, yes," Alex said, pained. If there was anything that Alex Hesse had ever wanted in his whole life, it was for Angela Arbogast to go far, far away, right this very second.

"Too bad." No way that was going to happen, Angela decided. *Je sui y je reste.* The phrase came back to her from her high school French. Here I am and here I stay. There was something very fishy about this guy, and especially about why he'd been staying here so long. Larry Arbogast wasn't exactly known for his hospitality. As gregarious as he was in a crowd, he didn't really care for people taken one at a time.

Angela noticed something else, too. The throw pillows on the couch were out of order; they were rumpled and crushed and not arranged in the sacred sequence—floral, houndstooth, *then* paisley. Also, there seemed to be somebody else on the floor behind the sofa.

Diana now popped up beside Alex and went through an elaborate and rather clumsy pantomime of putting a lost contact lens back into her eye. "Found it!" she crowed, and grinned a little foolishly.

The fact that this strange woman's blouse was buttoned up wrong and was hanging askew outside her skirt didn't ease Angela's suspicions. "Who's that?" she demanded.

Diana stood up, adjusting her clothing. "Dr. Diana Reddin," she said hastily. "I really must be going."

Alex's face crumpled in disappointment, and he tailed Diana to the door, begging like a dog. "No, please. I have a bedroom."

Diana shook her head no and gave him a quick peck on his cheek. "I'd love to see it some time. Talk to you soon." And she was gone.

Alex turned back to Angela, his face a disconsolate mask. Added to his loneliness and physical discomfort was now an overwhelming feeling of sexual frustration. He and Angela eyed each other, each of them checking out the other's burgeoning belly. Angela, of course, had no idea that Alex was pregnant; she only thought that he was fat, yet she felt that there was something about this Dr. Alexander Hesse that she couldn't quite figure out, something that rang a bell deep inside her.

"Would you like some chamomile tea?" Alex said invitingly.

"Uh . . ." Angela hesitated, then said, "Why not? Sure." She followed as Alex led the way into the kitchen.

"And I have the most delicious little butter cookies from Belgium."

An hour later, Angela and Alex were old friends, buddies united in chitchat and a love of food, any kind of food, including the piping hot greasy barbecue delivered by Uncle Soul and the big containers of Chinese food that the bicycle delivery man from Tong Tong in China-town brought to their door after a frantic, hungry telephone call. They had demolished almost everything, but were still perched on chairs at the kitchen table, tinkering with dessert. Empty and half-empty food wrappers and takeout containers stood all around them on the table and the kitchen counters. Their fingers and lips were smeared with barbecue sauce, and they were comfortably full, content with the world.

"I'll take another little smidgen of the Rocky Road," Angela said hungrily. Alex grabbed the container and scooped out his version of a "little smidgen," enough for three people, but Angela didn't protest. She dug into the huge bowl of ice cream while Alex poured his favorite, Cap'n Crunch, into his own bowl, topped it with a double handful of Whoppers, and poured milk over all. Milk was good for you, he thought, digging in. Junior needed calcium for teeth and bones.

"She seems very nice," said Angela, looking sideways at Alex. "Is it serious?"

Putting his spoon down, Alex chose his words carefully. "I'm at a particularly vulnerable stage in my life, so I'm taking it very slowly."

"That's smart," Angela nodded. "Any more spareribs?"

He passed her one and helped himself to one, and the two of them gnawed for a moment in companionable silence. Then Alex asked suddenly, "How about you . . . and the father?"

"Oh, I haven't even heard from him since it happened," Angela said with a little sigh.

"Bastard," Alex said empathetically. "Pass the coleslaw?" He took a big forkful directly out of the container and crammed it into his mouth, on top of the remains of the sparerib.

Angela shrugged. "I never expected to hear from him. And don't get me wrong, I couldn't be *happier* about being pregnant, but . . . being of . . . a certain age . . . single . . . it's tough."

"Tell me about it," said Alex with a nod. When he saw

Angela looking at him strangely, he added, "I mean . . . I can imagine. There's a wing left."

"Oh, okay." Angela helped herself and chewed on it thoughtfully. "Did anyone ever tell you that you eat like a pregnant woman?"

Alex swallowed hard. "I enjoy mixing cuisines," he said hastily.

Quite suddenly Angela gasped out loud and doubled over, clutching at her abdomen. In the same second, Alex grabbed at *his* belly and he, too, doubled with a grunt.

Angela let her breath out in a whoosh and sat upright again. "The baby pushed," she explained.

"Yes," said Alex, who had just experienced a particularly vigorous kick from Junior.

"What's wrong with *you*?"

"Sympathy pains," he said quickly.

Angela eyed him, then smiled. "I hardly know you. You must be a very sympathetic guy."

Alex nodded. "These days, yes," he said, in what must have been the understatement of the decade.

Six months pregnant, Alex Hesse couldn't get any of his trousers buttoned over his belly, and his shirts were popping their buttons. So Larry Arbogast bundled him up and drove him to the fat man's clothing store in the mall, a shop euphemistically titled Big Guy's Store. The awning over the entrance carried a welcome, "Hey, Big Guy!" and, underneath, the words "Clothing and Accessories for the Larger Lifestyle" appeared in curly letters.

Glumly, feeling humiliated, Alex stood with his hands hanging by his sides while Larry bustled from rack to rack, pulling off garments for Alex to try on. Poor Alex Hesse! How humiliating to have to shop here! No man

108

had ever had to try on maternity clothing before. The only bright spots in Alex's week had been the pig-out with Angela, about which he had wisely kept his mouth shut to Larry, and, much more important, his steamy necking session with the lovely Diana, about which he decided to confide in Larry. After all, Larry Arbogast was the closest thing to a best friend he had. He took the "maternity" clothing from his best friend's plump little paws and disappeared into a dressing room.

"I like her. I think she likes me, too."

"What makes you say that?" asked Larry, hanging around outside the dressing room, fidgeting impatiently. Alex came out wearing a loose, loud sport shirt and a voluminous pair of khaki trousers. Larry, who possessed a sense of aesthetics and a wardrobe full of custom-made Italian suits, winced at the sight. Alex looked like ten pounds of cow flop in a five-pound sack.

"She said she likes a little upholstery on a guy. And she kissed me."

Larry shrugged his shoulders. "Maybe she was just trying to be nice. They do that. Angela . . . we're in the lawyer's office signing the divorce papers . . . *her* idea, I might add . . . and she turns on the waterworks and it's 'Oh, Larry, where will I ever find a sweet soul like you?' And all the while she's signing right there on the dotted line. I mean, what is *that*?" he asked bitterly.

"Maybe she just likes me," Alex said, hurt. "Why are you always so negative?"

Larry grunted. "All right, say she really is madly in love with you. You're in *no* condition to start a relationship. At least give me that?"

A dreamily pensive expression came over Alex's face. "I'm starting to believe in fate," he murmured. "My baby, finding a compatible woman—it's all part of a design. Maybe I should see a psychic."

Helpless in the face of this irrationality, Larry could only shake his head. Alex peered at himself in the full-length mirror, depressed again. "I hate my body."

The store clerk, a portly little fellow wearing his own merchandise, hove into view, beaming cheerily. "Lookin' prosperous there!" he chortled, eyeballing Alex's protruding gut.

"Feels a little loose in the waist," said Alex.

"Better leave room to grow," Larry advised.

"Good idea."

"That's the spirit!" the clerk said brightly, and began to total up the sale as Alex, his expression downcast, studied his ungainly image in the looking glass.

On the way home, they stopped at a supermarket for groceries; it was little short of miraculous to Larry Arbogast how much food Alex wolfed down on a daily basis. Alex wasn't eating only for two—he was eating for two hundred.

Larry shopped carefully—fresh fruit, low-fat yogurt, salad greens, chicken breasts, orange juice, salmon steaks—everything to ensure good nutrition. Alex trailed after him, throwing his supplementary choices into the shopping cart—Ring Dings, Oreos, Devil Dogs, Count Chocula cereal, Cocoa Puffs to mix with the Count Chocula, Hershey chocolate syrup to drizzle over the mixed cereals—and while standing on line to check out, Alex added packages of beef jerky strips and Reese's Peanut Butter Cups from the impulse-purchase racks near the cash register. As a fillip, he threw in the *National Enquirer* and the *Star*. "I like the horoscopes," he explained when Larry glared at him.

Sighing, Larry shelled out $103.68. As they drove home, Alex expressed an interest in ice cream—big surprise!—and they drove to Ghiradelli Square, where they picked up a hand-packed quart of Double Fudge Rocky Road to hold the big guy through suppertime. When they got to Larry's house, the little guy unpacked the trunk of the Chrysler, piled his arms high with grocery sacks, and struggled under his burden up the front walk, while Alex followed behind, toting only the little freezer bag from the ice cream store.

Suddenly Alex gasped, grunted, and dropped the freezer bag.

"C'mon!" snapped Larry. "You can't even carry the ice cream?"

"Don't yell at me!" whined Alex defensively.

"I'm not yelling. *This is yelling!* Hear the difference?"

"Shut up," Alex winced. "Junior kicked again."

"Who?"

"Junior."

Larry paled. A sudden, very clear image entered his mind unbidden: a freezer opening with a nitrogen *whoosh,* a test tube clearly labeled "Junior." But how could Alex possibly know? Nah, it's gotta be a coincidence, Larry told himself.

"The book said to talk to the baby, and I don't know if it's a boy or girl, so I call it Junior. Why?"

"Nothing," Larry said shortly, but Alex scrutinized his face closely.

"*Something*," he retorted suspiciously. "You have that look."

Larry moved hastily to cover his tracks. "No, it's just . . . the guy I got the egg from? He called it Junior,

111

you know, joking. Funny coincidence." He juggled the grocery bags, which were heavy and starting to slip.

"Who was that guy?" Alex's brows drew together. "You said a colleague had an anonymous harvest."

"Colleague, yeah," Larry muttered, thinking fast.

"Do I know him?"

"Nah," Larry evaded. "You don't know him." It wasn't exactly a lie. Not exactly the truth, mind you, yet not exactly a lie, either. The donor wasn't a "him," it was a "her."

"How do you know?" Alex's curiosity was really aroused.

"I don't *know*," said Larry, squirming and beginning to sweat. "Uh, do you know . . . Stan, um, Mulwray?" There was no way that Alex could possibly know him, because Stan, um, Mulwray was a total figment of Larry's desperate imagination.

"No, I don't know him. Do we know anything about the donor egg?"

"No! It's anonymous, like I said." Larry's palms had begun to sweat, and it was hard for him to hold onto the groceries. "If you're up to it, could you get the door?" he complained, agitated. "I'm getting a hernia here."

Alex stepped up on the porch to open the door and saw with a start a tall figure sitting in one of the front porch chairs, half-hidden under a blossoming vine that over-hung the porch roof. It was Noah Banes, and his black eyes were glittering like two ripe olives.

"How very domestic," he purred smoothly. "All that's missing is the pitter-patter of little feet, no?"

Uh-oh. Alex glanced quickly at Larry, and Larry glanced quickly at Alex, and both of them felt the urgency of concealment, especially from this man.

"Banes," Larry said without warmth. "Forgotten, but not gone. What do *you* want?"

"Couldn't help overhearing." Banes smiled the smile of a hungry boa constrictor sighting a plump jerboa. "Something about a donor egg?"

Larry and Alex traded faux-baffled looks and carried the grocery bags into the house. Noah Banes unfolded his six feet six inches of curious pomposity and followed the two into the kitchen.

"Donor egg?" Alex echoed blandly.

"Don't know what you're talking about," said Larry with a shrug. They began to unpack the groceries.

"I *heard* you!" Banes protested.

Alex pretended to think. "Donor egg? Donor egg? Oh, *don't renege*! What you heard was 'don't renege.' We were discussing this deal we'd made—"

"About who would do the shopping and who would do the cooking." Larry jumped right in.

"And because he came along on the shopping, he said he shouldn't have to cook, and I was saying—"

"'Don't renege,'" finished Larry. "You know, on the deal."

Whew! Mentally, Larry and Alex wiped the sweat off their brows. That was too damn close. But was Banes buying it? He was still looking from one to the other with a suspicious expression.

"The lab printouts show you've been continuing Expectane production. Why am I in the dark, fellas?" Banes's tone was pleasant on the surface, but there was a detectible undercurrent of menace. He was a person to be reckoned with.

"Ah . . . uh . . ." fumpfed Alex. "We're closing out the chimp protocols."

Noah Banes smiled, a smile chilly enough to freeze fire. "Come on, guys, it's *me*! Who do you think you're dicking with? I checked with the primate lab. They said the chimps haven't been tested on since the project was terminated."

"The truth is . . . ," began Alex, then he ran into a stone wall. What was a credible lie? He glanced desperately at his more glib partner. "You tell him, Larry."

Larry Arbogast's brain was scampering around like a mouse on a wheel. "We . . . uh . . . we had a surplus of the steroid base, so rather than just let it go to waste, we just . . ."

"Completed the production run," supplied Alex. "We stockpiled Expectane for when the FDA *does* approve the clinical trials . . ."

"We weren't sure about the university policies. That's why the lie . . . fib." Larry was getting rattled.

"We're happy to make up for any budget overages," offered Alex with finality. *You want money? You got it. Case closed.*

But to Noah Banes the case was far from closed. He still fixed a fish-eyed stare on the two of them, and he wasn't convinced by the wimpish "don't renege" argument. He could have sworn the actual words he'd overheard were "donor egg."

The alarm on Alex's wristwatch went off suddenly and shrilly. *Beep. Beep. Beep.* It was time for the next dose of Expectane. "Excuse me," said Alex, and left the room.

"What's that about?" Noah Banes asked Larry.

"I don't know, Banes. What're you doing, writing a book?"

Banes's sharp eyes studied Alex going up the stairs, evidently in response to the timed alarm. Something was going on up there, something they didn't want him to know about. He turned to Larry, who was busy putting the groceries away, his nonchalance restored.

"You want to know what I think?" Banes asked coldly. "I think you two cowboys have an Expectane-assisted pregnancy under way, right here in this house."

Ooof! "Sorry, you're wrong," answered Larry, as coolly as he could.

Banes shook his head. "That hardly ever happens." Then he switched gears, assuming his oily, confidential manner. "Listen, Larry, I'm on *your* side. If you're coloring outside the lines here, I can *help*. The university board, the FDA—these are my people. I can talk to them. The important thing is the *work*."

Larry knew he would have to show a controlled confidence he did not feel. He turned from stashing away the Count Chocula and the peanut butter cups and looked Banes straight in the eye. Speaking slowly and with great emphasis, he said, "Noah, listen to me. I'm speaking English. *Nothing's going on.*"

Banes shook his head from side to side, in a pretense of disappointment. "How can I help if you insist on leaving me out of the loop?"

Having taken his dose of Expectane, Alex came back down the stairs. He glanced at Larry significantly, his look saying plainly, *What the hell is* he *still doing here?*

"Thanks for stopping by," Larry said with finality.

"See you around the campus," Alex said pleasantly. They ushered Banes to the door, but the university director wasn't quite ready to go. There was more to be learned here, so he tried to stall.

"Mind if I use the bathroom?"

"Right over there," Alex said and pointed. "Pick up the seat."

Noah Banes headed for the indicated first-floor bathroom as Larry and Alex went back into the kitchen to finish stowing away Alex's favorite sugar rushes.

"Think he believed us?" Alex asked in an undertone.

"There is no pregnant *woman*," said Larry with a shrug. "That's the truth."

Noah Banes stopped outside the bathroom and looked around. Larry and Alex were still busy in the kitchen and seemed to have forgotten him for the moment. Nobody was even glancing in his direction. This was Banes's chance, the golden opportunity to look around uninvited. He moved swiftly and silently up the stairs to the bedrooms on the second floor.

The first bedroom he checked out seemed to belong to Larry. The suits in the closet were all 44 short. Banes looked around quickly and saw nothing unusual, so he moved down the corridor to the next bedroom, like Goldilocks in the house of the three bears.

They might be keeping a pregnant woman stashed here, because this was obviously a woman's bedroom, to judge from the flowered wallpaper, the flowered drapes, the flowered cushions, the flowered— Wait, hold the phone! Bingo! Arranged on the dresser was just what Banes was looking for: fetal monitors, medical instruments, a blood pressure sphygmomanometer, a stethoscope—the works. This was definitely where those two liars must have her holed up, the woman they were using to test Expectane. Wonder how much they're paying her? Banes thought.

She had to be up here somewhere, because Alex's alarm had beeped, and obviously he had had to rush upstairs to take care of her needs. There was an attached bathroom, with a closed door. She was in there, had to be.

"Come out, come out, wherever you are," said Banes under his breath, and he whipped open the door. Nobody. The bathroom was empty.

All right, so she wasn't here at this precise moment. To any snoop worthy of the name, a bathroom is a fertile feeding ground. A medicine chest can prove to be a cornucopia of information, a deep peep into the private life of the body and soul. Noah Banes would never forgive himself if he didn't catalog everything in the little cabinet.

Bottles of prenatal vitamins—that was incriminating, but not unexpected. The giant-sized bottle of Tums, obviously dipped into. Yes, of course, and more? Banes opened a lower drawer and lifted out an intriguing steel case. He put it on the marble sink top and opened it. This was more like it. It was filled with little stoppered vials. Taking one out, he held it up to the light, looked it over, opened it, sniffed at the contents. Interesting.

Banes recapped and pocketed the vial and was turning to go when his eye fell on the wastebasket, another bonanza for any ambitious snoop. A number of empty bottles were in the basket, and Noah Banes pocketed one of them. A little comparison, a little laboratory analysis, and proof positive. If the empty vial matched in contents the full one, then somebody in this room was definitely taking the compound. And Banes would bet his best bow tie from Chipp that the mystery compound was Expectane.

He'd gotten pretty much what he'd come for. Noah Banes caught sight of himself in the dresser mirror and smiled in satisfaction. Damn, he was good!

Chapter Seven

Junior

Alex stared into the mirror, not too unhappy with his reflection. He turned this way and that, preening. He was dressed to kill in a good-looking double-breasted suit that went a long way to disguising his big pregnant belly. Not too shabby, he thought, giving his new silk necktie from Italy a twitch to straighten it. He checked out his hair, bared his teeth to make certain they were clean and shining, and tore himself away from the glass. He took a clean handkerchief out of his top dresser drawer and left the room.

Thwack! Thwack! Out in the hallway he heard a noise. It was a peculiar noise which Alex hadn't heard before. He couldn't identify it, but it seemed to be coming from Larry's bedroom. Curious, he stuck his head around the door.

"I'm taking Diana to dinner. I'll see you later," he announced.

"Yeah, later." Larry was sitting glumly on his bed, tossing darts at a poster on the wall. *Thwack! Thwack!* Still curious, Alex came in and took a look at the poster, which pictured a long-haired rock-and-roll band in full cry.

"Who's that?" All rock-and-roll musicians looked alike to Alex.

"Aerosmith," said Larry through gritted teeth, as he aimed another dart at the bass guitarist.

"You don't like their music?" asked Alex, baffled.

Larry Arbogast's face struggled between rage and unhappiness, and unhappiness won out. "Seven years I tried *everything*," he complained bitterly. "I couldn't get Angela pregnant. One of these clowns . . . one night . . . one *shot* . . . mission accomplished. It's just not fair." Two darts in quick succession slammed into the poster. *Thwack! Thwack!*

Alex Hesse studied the poster, taking in the tight jeans, the waist-length hair, the stage makeup. Somehow he couldn't picture the petite, fastidious, fussy little Angela with one of those grungy behemoths. "Which one?"

Larry tossed another dart and sighed dispiritedly. "I don't know. Doesn't matter." But it obviously did.

Alex felt a rush of sympathy for the little guy. He'd never thought of Larry Arbogast as having personal problems, but why not? Even though he avoided intimacy like yellow fever, Larry was nearly as human as the next fellow. "Do you still love her?" Alex asked softly.

"No, no," Larry answered without conviction. "It's good it's over. It's just that this baby thing's got me a little . . . you know . . . I'm having some *feelings,* that's all. It's *good* it's over. I'll see you later, okay?" Turning away from Alex, he pegged another dart at the poster. Bull's-eye, but it brought Larry little satisfaction.

Larry needed a friend; should Alex stay? He felt torn. Part of him wanted to be a friend, to remain here with the little guy and give him what comfort he could, but most of him—the strongest part—was dragging him by the collar out the door to meet Diana. He'd talk to Larry later, he decided. There was plenty of time.

As soon as he came out the front door to get into his taxi, which was already waiting outside at the curb, Angela Arbogast came screeching up in her red Mercedes. She slammed on the parking brake.

"Is he home?" she demanded, without even saying hello. She was visibly distraught.

"Yes." It's a good thing I decided to go, thought Alex. Perhaps Angela's visit would do Larry some good. Perhaps if they spent some time together . . .

"Alone?"

"Very."

She waddled to the front door. Forgetting Larry, Alex got into his cab, His mind was now only on Diana. He was meeting her at a popular Tuscan bistro in Telegraph Hill, and he was looking forward to this evening with every fiber of his burgeoning being. He *needed* a real evening out, with an attractive woman. No, scratch that. Not with just any woman. With Diana, only with Diana.

The evening got off to a good start. Alex was a few minutes early, and Diana was exactly on time. She was lovelier than he had ever seen her, wearing something shimmering that set her hair and eyes aglow. Their table was a good one, well placed, with wide, comfortable chairs for which Alex, who was finding it increasingly difficult to squeeze into tight spaces, was almost pathetically grateful. The tablecloth and napkins were snowy white; the flowers in their little earthenware jug were fragrant and fresh. The menu was impressive, large and varied, and everything on it sounded delicious. As soon as they were seated, a waiter rushed over to set down warm focaccia bread and herb-flavored olive oil for dipping, and the starving Alex happily demolished all of it.

Diana made pleasant conversation while Alex ordered vast quantities of food and chose a wine. Smiling, she chitchatted about what was going on in her laboratory and her progress with the Ovum Cryogenics Project while they waited for their food, but it was when their entrées were laid before them—lobster in the shell for Diana, a veal chop with pasta and spinach for Alex—that it all began to fall apart.

"Your calamari will be right out," the waiter assured Alex, who only nodded with his mouth full. He was already busy emptying his plate. Diana regarded him for a moment and then she spoke the fateful words.

"I'm a little confused about this *strudelhund* thing you've got," she said, not unpleasantly.

Uh-oh, Alex thought. This doesn't sound good. Alex stopped chewing and looked up from his veal chop. "How so?" he asked with caution.

Diana drew in a deep breath, and her face was troubled as she began. "Well, to be perfectly blunt, no one's ever heard of it. It's not in any of the journals, and the pathologists I contacted came up empty-handed as well. And what's more, there is no Gelandesprung, Austria."

Oh, boy. Alex swallowed his food with an effort not to choke on it and looked across the table at Diana, who sat back in her chair, regarding him with a quizzical expression. She had gone to a lot of trouble to check up on his condition. She had caught him fair and square in a series of stupid lies; now he had nothing to say.

For an instant, Alex wished Larry were here, with his glib tongue and fertile brain. But no, no, he didn't wish for that at all. Reason took over, and he felt actually relieved. For six months Alex had lied to Diana. He hated lying, and here suddenly was his golden chance to stop the deception and come clean. Suddenly he wanted to come clean to Diana Reddin more than anything he'd ever wanted in his life. He wanted to share his wonderful secret with her; he longed to tell her about Junior. She was a woman as well as a scientist in the field of human reproduction; surely Diana, if anybody, would understand and be happy for him. And who knows? Maybe his secret, an intimacy shared, would bring them closer together. He longed for the closeness with all his heart.

Meanwhile he had to think of a way to tell her the truth about his pregnancy that wouldn't freak Diana out and send her screaming from the restaurant, no doubt knocking down a couple of waiters in her haste to get away from him.

"Alex?" Diana broke the silence, and Alex realized it really was time for him to speak.

"You're right. I'm sorry I had to deceive you."

"What's going on?" asked Diana.

He leaned over the table, and spoke in a low, confidential tone. "Can I really talk to you? About anything?"

"Sure you can," said Diana with a smile. It's about time, she thought. Let's get these lies behind us so that we can start fresh.

"I want you to know everything about me," Alex said seriously.

"Likewise." Diana tucked into her lobster, tearing at the shell to get at the succulent meat. She ripped off a claw, which slipped out of her grasp and went flying through the air to land on the next table. The diners handed it back.

"Thank you." She leaned across to Alex, so that their noses nearly touched. "I'll go first." And she told him her deepest secret. "I'm a little clumsy. No, really. There.

Now it's your turn." She searched his face for shock and horror, but didn't find it.

Alex sat back in his chair. "Can you keep an open mind?"

"I think so," Diana said.

"Really *wide* open?"

"Alex . . ." Reaching across the table, she touched his hand encouragingly and smiled into his eyes. *Tell me, you can tell me, don't be afraid,* she signaled with her glance. He steeled himself and summoned up all his courage.

"I have a most extraordinary condition," he began, just as their waiter brought a plate of fried calamari rings and set it on the table. "Thank you."

The tiny momentary distraction changed the course of his thoughts, and the course of the evening, and very possibly the course of both their lives. When Alex resumed his confession, it was with a roundabout approach, a question. "Are you familiar with the work of Edward Jenner?" he asked.

"Yes," Diana nodded. "He invented vaccination."

"And confirmed his findings by experimenting on himself," Alex went on.

"Right."

Alex leaned in close to Diana. "Have you ever been tempted to apply the fruits of your research to your own life?" This was the best way to tell her; stress the scientific, compare his own experiments with Jenner's.

"Well, sure," she said and nodded again. "In fact, I have."

Alex sat back, surprised. "You have? How?"

Diana cast her eyes down, suddenly modest. "Nothing

so extraordinary as Jenner. I used my cryogenic technique to freeze one of my own eggs."

"You did? Why?"

Diana looked sheepish suddenly. "Well, I've always wanted children, but I never found the man I wanted to raise them with. And I'm not getting any younger, so . . . I froze one of my own eggs, in case Mr. Right came along too late. It's in my dairy section, labeled 'Junior.'"

Junior! Had he heard her correctly? "Wh-what did you say?" asked Alex falteringly.

"My egg. It's in the freezer at the lab."

"You called it . . . Junior?" Alex found it difficult to get the words out.

"Well," Diana said matter-of-factly, not realizing that she was causing another San Francisco earthquake right here at the table, "I didn't want to label it with my own name. Everyone would know, and you can't tell if it's going to be a boy or a girl, so I just called it 'Junior.'"

"Junior?" croaked Alex again. It was all too much. His mind went reeling, stunned by the possibility that . . . No, it couldn't be . . . Larry had sworn . . . but Larry always lied, didn't he? Larry was a well-known, accomplished liar. Conflicting thoughts pounded at Alex's brain. It was a coincidence, had to be a coincidence. Wasn't it? Alex turned pale and began feeling sick. All he could think of was getting home and confronting Larry Arbogast, making Larry tell him the truth. He had to know the truth about Junior.

"Enough about me, this is embarrassing," laughed Diana. "Tell me what you're up to!"

Alex stood up in a daze and dropped his napkin into the calamari. For a moment he rocked back and forth on his feet, not knowing whether or not he was going to faint. "I'm . . . I'm sorry . . . I have to leave," he gasped.

"Alex! What's wrong?" Concerned, Diana could only stare at him. He *did* look ill.

But he didn't answer, only waddled quickly for the exit. Alex left with his secret still intact, although he had just been given an explosive piece of information that he couldn't yet deal with. Diana was sitting there with her mouth open, waiting for an explanation of his odd behavior. But what could Alex possibly say to her—*I'm having your baby*?

Meanwhile, back in Larry's house, Angela was stretched out on the dining room floor, with her shirt up, tapping a spoon against her bare, bulging belly. "*Now* listen!" she cried, distraught.

Larry placed his stethoscope on her belly and listened through the earpieces.

"Nothing, right?" demanded Angela.

"Angela, cut it out," Larry said with weary patience. "That doesn't mean *anything*!"

"She's *deaf*! I just know it! And watch this!" She shimmied her belly from side to side. It shook like Jell-O, then came to a quivering rest. "Not a roll, not a kick, not in two days! Don't tell me she's just a heavy sleeper!"

"They don't respond on cue," sighed Larry.

"She did! And now she's not!" wailed Angela, afraid for her baby. "Something's wrong, I just *know* it!"

Thoroughly exasperated, Larry threw up his hands. "Okay, you're right. Is that what you want to hear? All those drugs the father took probably messed her up good."

Angela looked blank. "What drugs?"

Larry uttered a snort of contempt. "I read up on Aerosmith. Wasted for a *decade*! Coke, pills, booze . . ."

"What are you talking about?" Angela raised herself on her elbows to stare at him, totally stymied.

There was the sudden noise of a commotion outside, but Larry paid no attention. This was much more important. Larry was finally going to get at the truth. "Which one is he?" he demanded.

Oh, now she understood. Now everything was clear. "He's not in the *band*," said Angela. "Is *that* what you thought, that he was in the band?"

Oh, now he didn't understand. "Well, yeah," said Larry, confused. "You said—"

"That he was on tour with them. He's their *personal trainer*." Angela shot him an impatient look, then suddenly her saucer eyes widened to the size of dinner plates and she cried out. "Oh! Larry, she kicked! She's alive!" She was suddenly bursting with happiness.

That was the exact moment when Alex finally got the front door open and stormed in, making a beeline for Larry. Steam was pouring out of his ears, and his eyes were flashing sparks. Angela yelped like a puppy and pulled her shirt down over her belly.

"I want to talk to you!" Alex growled and grabbed hold of Larry, dragging him out of the dining room and into the kitchen like a sack of potatoes, and propping him up against the kitchen counter. "Where did you get Junior?!" he demanded, his jaw so firmly set it looked like boulders.

"I told you!" cried Larry.

So angry he didn't stop to consider what he was doing, Alex lifted Larry off the floor and shook him as a bear shakes a honey tree. "The truth this time!" he roared. "We're talking about my baby!"

His little feet dangling in midair, Larry looked the moment of truth in the face and recognized it. "All right, all right," he capitulated. "Keep your voice down. I got it from Reddin's lab."

Dr. Diana Reddin's Ovum Cryogenics Project. There it was, the confirmation Alex had both expected and dreaded. "It's Diana's!" he growled.

Larry's mouth opened in disbelief. "You mean . . . hers *personally*?"

"Yes," Alex retorted grimly.

Uh-oh. "Uh-oh, sorry."

Sorry? *Sorry?!* Sorry didn't quite cut it. "You were supposed to get an *anonymous* egg," Alex yelled.

"Shhhhh!" Larry put a finger to his lips and glanced into the nearby dining room, where Angela was no doubt listening intently. He pulled Alex into the living room, out of earshot. "I tried. Everyone was all out."

Alex snapped, losing his temper. "Can't you do *anything* right?!" he demanded.

"Look, don't start with me." Larry's temper also flared up hotly, and he raised his voice. "If you'd stopped taking the Expectane back when you were supposed to, it wouldn't even be an issue!"

"What a horrible thing to say!" gasped Alex, shocked.

"Well, it's the truth! This was *your* idea, not mine! Women have such convenient memories when they're pregnant."

"Take it back!" Alex cried fiercely. He sank into an

armchair, lifted up his shirt and scratched at his bulging belly.

"Freudian slip," Larry conceded. "I know you're not a real woman."

"No, not that. The part about I should have ended it. Junior heard you. Take it back."

Larry rolled his eyes in exasperation. "Oh, for chrissakes! Okay, I take it back," he said grumpily.

"Say it like you mean it," insisted Alex stubbornly.

The big dweeb. Larry shook his head with something like affection. "Sorry, Junior," he said to the naked belly. "All right?"

Alex suddenly winced. "Oooh, it's kicking. Come and feel," he invited.

"I don't think so." Larry took a backward step and shook his head with vehemence.

The baby kicked again, hard. "Aiiiieeee!" yelled Alex. "Come on. We need a healing experience, the three of us," he said to wheedle Larry.

"Gimme a break!" wailed Larry, who was allergic to Kodak moments.

"Just do it!" snapped Alex, suddenly looking every inch of his masculine six feet four. Reluctantly Larry placed a hand on Alex's swollen belly. "Just a second," murmured Alex. "There! Did you feel it?"

There was a gasp from the doorway, and Larry snatched his hand away as though it were on fire. Alex quickly pulled his shirt down and both men turned to see Angela, stunned, staring at them in horror.

"Larry!" yelled Angela. "What the hell is going on?!"

"What? Nothing," Larry answered, turning red and looking guilty.

"You were *touching* him! Oh, God! Oh, no! I can't deal with this!"

"Deal with what?" A suspicion crossed Larry's mind. Hey, what the hell was she thinking? True, this *was* San Francisco, but even so . . .

"You two are a . . . twosome?" Angela could barely get her mouth around the word.

At the same instant, both men exploded in denials.

Alex: "What?! No no no no no no no!"

Larry: "Who whoa whoa whoa *whoa!*"

"What's going on?" demanded Angela furiously.

The truth was the only way out. "He's . . . well . . . he's pregnant," said Larry.

"I'm going to be a mama, too," Alex smiled proudly. His gap-toothed grin was the clincher.

Angela froze while her mind tried to process the information just handed to her. She looked at Larry, at his guileless expression. She looked at Alex's big bulging belly. She looked again at the shit-eating blissful gap-toothed grin on the big dweeb's face. She remembered Alex's empathy, his doubling over and grabbing his abdomen, the pig-out in the kitchen. *Did anyone ever tell you you eat like a pregnant woman?* she'd said. Somehow, subconsciously maybe, she must have known. All of these thoughts flooded through her mind in a split second, the split second before everything went black, and Angela Arbogast sank to the floor in a dead faint.

It was too bad for Noah Banes that he couldn't have been a fly on the wall when Larry and Alex were telling Angela the truth. He wouldn't have had to go to the trouble and expense of commissioning laboratory analyses of the vials he'd found in the upstairs bedrooms in Larry

Arbogast's house. Even so, he'd made real progress in unraveling the fabric of lies spun by those two fakers.

"You're *sure* it's Expectane?" He whirled from his office window, where he had been pacing back and forth, his hands clasped behind his back.

"Absolutely," said his assistant, Samantha. "We compared what you gave us with a sample we had on file in the lab."

Banes did a little impromptu victory jig, not a pretty sight. "Who did they think they were dealing with? That's what really hurts. Well, let's find out who she is—"

"Mr. Banes, there's something else," Samantha said. "That sample you gave us? It was part Expectane, *and* part female hormones. Estrogens and progesterone, to be exact."

"Well, wouldn't that be consistent with an assisted pregnancy?" asked Banes.

Samantha shook her head doubtfully. "Not a dosage of this size. It's more like the amount you'd take, say, preparing for a sex-change operation."

Banes glanced idly out of his office window, and an extraordinary thing happened. He noticed Alex Hesse get out of a taxicab, pay it off, and begin to lumber toward the Lufkin Center and Diana's laboratory, cradling his cumbersome belly in his large hands.

If Isaac Newton had not been sitting under an apple tree when the pippins were ripe enough to fall, we might not be obeying the laws of gravity today. If Noah Banes had not been looking out of his office window at the precise moment that Samantha spoke the words "sex change," and had not seen Dr. Alexander Hesse waddling along on swollen feet, looking completely, totally, unmistakably pregnant, the penny would not have dropped.

But the penny did drop, and with it everything else dropped into place. "Oh, my God!" gasped Banes, overcome by the enormity of the revelation. Of course, it was brilliant, brilliant! The Food and Drug Administration had denied Dr. Hesse and Dr. Arbogast permission to test Expectane on a *woman*, but they never mentioned anything about a *man*!

Diana's lab was a hive of activity when Alex came in. Diana was in a huddle with her lab assistants, Jenny and Arthur, around a computer terminal. In Alex's old corner, his own lab assistant, Alice, was typing at the keyboard, while the chimpanzees, Minnie and Moe, were standing at the sink, washing up the glass laboratory beakers. Their adorable little baby chimp, Michelle, kept getting in their way.

Alex's entrance was the cause of mixed reactions. Loyal Alice stood up and saluted. The apes climbed all over him happily, Minnie paying particular attention to Alex's belly, which she openly admired. Only Dr. Diana Reddin shot him a dirty look.

"We're busy," she said shortly.

"Please. I need to talk to you," begged Alex.

"You need to *apologize* to me." Diana's voice dripped frost.

"I'm sorry," Alex apologized. "Please, Diana, let me explain." For the first time he noticed Arthur and Jenny hanging around looking uncomfortable. "Take five, guys," he told them, and they made themselves scarce, leaving Alex alone with Diana in this corner of the lab.

Diana looked at Alex expectantly. For a long moment, he weighed the various approaches to telling her, and then he blurted simply, "I'm pregnant."

Seconds ticked by while Diana simply stared at him, disbelieving. Then, she gasped out, *"What?"*

Alex nodded gravely. "I really am pregnant." He drew his breath in deeply. "I tested Expectane on myself. We fertilized an egg and implanted it in my abdomen. Assisted by the drug and hormone supplements, I'm now seven months to term." He lifted up his shirt, and she got a good look at his taut, swollen, seven-months-pregnant belly.

Astonished, Diana could do nothing but stare, first at the belly, then at Alex's face. He nodded again. Still in shock, she moved away from him.

"Oh, my God!" she breathed. Reaching over gingerly, Diana poked a tentative finger at his belly, as though testing it to see if it was real. It was real.

"Oh, my God!" she gasped again.

"There's more," Alex said, his face troubled.

"More?!"

This was going to be the really hard part. Alex swallowed, then got the words out. "Larry was supposed to find an anonymous egg. He couldn't, so he . . . borrowed one . . . from your dairy section. It's . . . Junior."

Diana's face went white, and her voice emerged in a squeak. *"My* Junior?"

"Well," said Alex in a very soft voice, *"our* Junior, now."

Now the blood returned to Diana Reddin's cheeks as she erupted in fury. "You arrogant son of a bitch!" she yelled. She raised her fists to pummel him, but remembered in the nick of time that one doesn't pummel a pregnant wo— pregnant man. But Diana's strong feelings demanded relief, so she stomped on his foot, hard.

Alex yelped with pain, alarming loyal Alice, who stood up, ready to intervene and protect her boss. The chimps howled with laughter. "Please, don't be angry," Alex begged.

"Don't be *angry?!*" Diana fumed, "You *lie* to me, you *steal* from me, you take away my dignity and mock my very *womanhood* with your stupid, pigheaded, utterly selfish stunt! What am I supposed to be, *grateful*? This is just *so male!*" And, to ventilate her anger, she stomped on his foot again, even harder this time.

Alex winced in pain, but Diana's words were far more painful to him than her sharp heels in his instep. "I'm sorry," he pleaded sincerely. "The last thing I'd ever want to do is hurt you."

But Diana was not in the mood to hear any apologies from the man who was carrying her child, *her* child. "What did you think you were *doing*?" she hollered.

Alex had never before heard Diana raise her voice; it was always cool, clipped, elegant, teddibly British, but now she sounded exactly like Angela yelling at Larry, or like any really angry woman who's had it up to here. "As if men don't hold enough cards, you have to take *this* from us, too?! You are so *pitiful!*"

Before Alex could calm Diana down, the laboratory doors burst open, and Noah Banes, flanked by two burly security guards, burst in. He was grinning from ear to ear, and when he caught sight of Alex, his eyes lighted up and his grin stretched around the sides of his face and joined at the back of his head. He advanced on Alex with his right hand out.

"Let me shake the hand of the man who would be Mom!" he cried exultantly.

Alex backed away, alarmed. "What are you talking about?" he said hoarsely.

The man who would be Mom? Alex's lab assistant stared, aghast, as the realization hit her. It was the last piece of a puzzle that Alice had been ruminating over for months. Dr. Hesse's mystery illness, his localized weight gain, his mood swings, his frequent heartburn, loose sweatshirts—suddenly they all added up. Her boss was pregnant; he would be the first man in the history of the world to have a baby. Alice was deeply moved and very proud.

"Only the greatest scientific breakthrough in the history of this university! Bravo, Doctor!" Banes grabbed hold of Alex's right hand and pumped it enthusiastically.

"Leave me alone," pleaded Alex.

"Sorry," Banes said and grinned. "We're in this together now." He reached into the pocket of his academic tweed jacket and whipped out a contract, brandishing it in the air. " 'Exploitation of results,' " he read out loud triumphantly, " 'including but not limited to any and all procedures and patents resulting from university-funded research and development shall be at the sole discretion of the university!' " Which meant, of course, at the sole discretion of Noah Banes. He beckoned to Alex. "Come on, I've ordered some tests."

A look of horror crossed Alex's face, and he backed away. At once his loyal little crew moved forward to defend him, Alice wielding a large beaker menacingly and the chimps flanking him, showing their large, sharp teeth and making threatening simian noises.

"Leave me alone!" Alex cried again, this time in a deep growl.

"He said to leave him alone!" echoed Alice.

"Escort Dr. Hesse to the ambulance," Banes ordered crisply, and the two security guards moved forward toward Alex in a pincer movement. A little clumsily because of his bulk, Alex dodged past them, evading their grasp.

"Stop it!" cried Diana frantically. "He's . . . in a very delicate condition!" She began to push Banes away, not very effectively, but with enormous sincerity.

"*Et tu*, Diana?" Banes was so affected that even in the middle of bedlam he could dredge up Shakespeare's small Latin. "Get him!" he yelled at the guards.

The security guards' pincer closed in on Alex, and they grabbed him, one clinging to each of his arms.

"*No!*" Alex roared.

"You're university property now," said Noah Banes.

But Alex Hesse was a lot more powerful than they realized. Even though he was a laboratory scientist and seven months pregnant, he was big and muscular and as strong as a bull, and when he moved now, it was with lightning speed. Shaking off both guards, he lunged at Banes, sending him sprawling with one blow of his right fist.

"*My* body, *my* choice!" he shouted.

"*Yessss!*" echoed the feminist Alice, and the chimpanzees swung into action. Moe jumped on the back of one of the guards, covering his eyes so that the man couldn't see. Minnie grabbed the other guard by the testicles, digging her sharp little fingers into his short and curlies. The security guard let out a yowl of agony and crumpled to the floor, giving Alex the opportunity to hightail it out of there, an opportunity he did not miss.

He lumbered out of the laboratory and down the corridor of the Lufkin Center, weaving his way through knots of teachers and students. Banes, the security guards, Diana, Alice, and the three chimps followed hard on his heels. Alex careened through the exit doors, crashing right into a lab assistant carrying a rack of glass beakers. The beakers went flying in all directions, coming down in a shower of broken glass.

Alex tore across the campus like a quarterback with the ball, while Diana and the chimps did their best to run interference for him, blocking Banes and the guards, who were gaining on him.

With a screech of brakes, Larry Arbogast's Chrysler appeared out of nowhere and pounded to a stop at the curb. Larry leaned on the horn, honking furiously. Alex heard it and switched direction, heading for the car. Larry threw the door open, and Alex jumped into the front seat. He yelled out at Banes, "Don't mess with Mama!" and Larry peeled rubber, taking off like a bat out of Carlsbad.

Alex turned back to look out of the window; Banes was pitching a fit at the curb. Alex sank back into his seat, hyperventilating. Now that it was all over, a reaction to that huge rush of adrenaline set in, and Alex began to tremble all over. His breath came with difficulty, and he panted loudly.

"Easy, easy," cautioned Larry. "Take deep breaths."

"It was so scary," gasped Alex.

"There, there, it's okay. We've got to hide you."

Yes, hide. "Where?!" Alex wanted to know.

"I'm thinking . . . I'm thinking," muttered Larry, then his face brightened. Grinning, he reached for the car phone.

Chapter Eight

Casitas Madres

"This is everything I could get my hands on," said Angela doubtfully, handing over an overnight bag, a couple of dress bags, and a wig box. "I hope some of it'll work."

"Thanks, Angela, you're a lifesaver," Larry said gratefully, stowing the bags in his car.

"You're welcome." She turned to Alex. "How long will you be gone?"

Alex shook his head. "I'm not sure, a couple of weeks, maybe."

Angela laid a friendly hand on his big bicep. "Who am I going to chow down with?" she asked ruefully.

Alex smiled significantly. "Larry's gotten pretty used to it. And he's become quite the inventive chef."

"Come on, Alex. Thanks again, Angela," said Larry, embarrassed by Alex's compliment and Angela's moist looks. It wasn't hard to tell where this conversation was headed, and although he wasn't entirely unhappy with Alex's words or Angela's affectionate glances, they had more urgently pressing business to take care of.

They drove south from San Francisco on the twisting, scenic Pacific Coast Highway, past mountains and forests, past Santa Cruz, Monterey Bay, Big Sur, with the ocean on their right, down toward Carmel. Larry said little, concentrating on his driving. Alex watched the magnificent California coastal scenery speeding past the window, but his thoughts were elsewhere.

He was brooding about Diana, remembering when she had visited him at Larry's house and told him that she felt a strange kind of connection to him and concern for him; she had asked if perhaps they knew each other from earlier in their lives. He understood now what neither of them could have understood then, that the mystical connection she was feeling was for the baby he was carrying, for Junior. Her Junior as well as his. Somehow her body had spoken to her and told her that an important part of herself was inside Alex. Did she, too, understand the answer to that mystery now? Did she realize that the feelings they shared were the closest that a man and a woman can know? Did she share his belief that Fate herself was drawing them together in the most inevitable way?

Or was she still mad as hell at him?

"Diana said that I was selfish and arrogant, and that we'd taken away her dignity and the sacred role of womanhood," Alex said sadly.

"Isn't that typical?" Larry uttered a short, sour laugh. "I can't tell you how many times I've heard a pregnant woman complain 'I just wish a man could go through this.' You finally *do* it, and what do you get? Attitude and insults!"

Alex nodded, and the two drove on in silence for another hour, each man lost in his own thoughts. At last they turned off the highway, down a winding road lined in blossoming jacaranda trees, to a pebbled driveway that led to the gate of Casitas Madres.

Casitas Madres, a sprawling complex built in the

Spanish mission style characteristic of California, was made of white stucco with low-hanging roofs of red tile, and wrought-iron accents such as cunning lanterns and curlicued gates. Tall agapanthus grew in the colorful gardens outside the walls, and olive trees dropped ripe fruit for the birds. They drove under a trellised arch overgrown with silver-leaved ivy, and a hanging sign that read "Casitas Madres" in rustic lettering and rather coyly depicted a blissful mother cradling a happy infant. The car stopped at a guardhouse, and a cheerful female voice issued from the intercom box.

"Good afternoon. Checking in?"

"Yes," responded Larry. "Ms. Alexandra Hesse?"

"Welcome to Casitas Madres, Alexandra," said the voice. "Reception's in the main house, right up there to your left."

Larry drove on. Alex peered at himself in the rearview mirror and asked hesitantly, "Do I look all right?"

Larry braced himself and took a gander at the big guy. Alex was decked out in a woman's wig and clothing that looked really odd on his huge frame. His face was powdered and rouged, his lips outlined in bright lipstick, and he wore large hoop errings. He resembled the dog's dinner, several hours after it's brought back up from inside the dog.

"Avoid direct sunlight," Larry advised. He drove his car over a rustic little bridge and past an outdoor art class and pulled the Chrysler in to park in front of the impeccably landscaped main house. Wind chimes were tinkling in the afternoon breezes, and the clipped lawn looked like lush green velvet. A group of very pregnant women walked by slowly, holding hands and moving in a chain. Casitas Madres was, to put it crudely, a home for unwed mothers, but it was a very glitzy and criminally expensive home for unwed mothers from wealthy families.

Alex gave himself one last anxious inspection in the mirror, his large face apprehensive under its garish makeup. Larry eyeballed the passing women and grimaced. "Ms. Alexandra Hesse" would fit in here about as well as a rhinoceros would fit in a beehive.

"Jeez," he breathed. "You're sure you're okay with this?"

"Not a lot of choice," sighed Alex.

"You want to go over the rap again?" offered Larry. Anything to delay the unavoidable moment when they'd have to actually get out of the car and expose Alex's disguise to the incredulous derision of the world.

"No." Alex shook his head, resigned. "I know it."

"Okay, then, let's go."

The car door opened, and Alex Hesse stepped out, patting his wig and slipping on a pair of large sunglasses. A loud-patterned printed caftan, something like a circus tent with flowers, swirled around him and billowed in the breeze.

A female employee came out of the main house and took the suitcases out of the car trunk. Out of the corner of her eye, she got a surreptitious look at the six-foot-four brontosaurus in the caftan, but her well-trained face didn't break into an expression of either laughter or disgust. Still, she was forced to stifle a grin when Alex's head slammed into the overhanging wind chimes.

The receptionist in the entry hall of the main house was as manicured and glossy as the lawn outside, and she did not have the benefit of the sidelong glance. She had to encounter Alex in all his glory—full-frontal ugliness.

Little wonder that when she looked up from her computer, she was stunned almost to speechlessness.

While Alex patted his wig with nervous fingers, Larry whipped his credit card out and put it on the counter. "Alexandra Hesse, checking in?"

"W-we-welcome to Casitas Madres, Alexandra," the receptionist stammered. Flustered, she turned back to her keyboard, punching up the Hesse reservation, but she couldn't help stealing glances at the monstrously hulking figure in the billowing caftan.

"Is something the matter?" Larry asked blandly.

"No no. No no no . . . ," the receptionist answered nervously, and diverted her curious glance elsewhere.

By this time, a couple of the Casitas Madres staff members, trying to act natural, had sidled over for a closer look. When Alex turned to look back, they all pretended to be busy with little chores in the immediate neighborhood. Another woman, fiftyish, neatly dressed, maternal and kindly, came out of her office adjacent to the reception desk. With great poise, she quickly covered her astonishment on seeing Alex, glanced at the computer screen for the name, and extended her right hand graciously.

"Ms. Hesse? I'm Naomi Bender, director here at Casitas Madres. Welcome."

Alex took her hand, shook it with surprising delicacy, and answered her in a high, soft voice. "Thank you."

"Why don't we have a seat in the living room?" suggested the director. She led them into a large yet cosy room nearby, furnished with comfortable chairs and sofas, bowls of fresh flowers, and hanging plants blooming profusely in the spotless windows. There was a gleam of copper here and there and, of course, the inevitable Spanish wrought-iron touches. They sat down. A number of the staffers surreptitiously moved into eavesdrop position.

"I realize that my appearance may be a bit startling," Alex began softly, looking down at his hands.

Naomi cleared her throat and smiled brightly, and the subtle little incline of her head said plainly, "Well, now that you mention it—"

Alex looked up, his face a study in brave vulnerability, or vulnerable braveness, your choice. "If I may speak to your concerns?" he continued in that same soft, high voice. "When I was sportswoman with the East German Olympic track and field team, they dispensed the ana-bolic steroids as freely as here in America they dole out the Gatorade. Nothing was mentioned of the side effects which are so . . . obviously, painfully apparent."

Here Alex stopped, to stifle a sob and pull himself together, then he looked Naomi full in the face from behind his sunglasses. "But I am all woman," he assured her, lying through the lipstick on his teeth.

"Believe you me," put in Larry, rather coarsely.

"I'm almost eight months pregnant, and my Larry has to be traveling on business . . ."

"I can't stand to think of her, helpless and all alone," said Larry mournfully, with a soft, tender glance at his "Alexandra."

"Please, Naomi, I may look . . . different . . . but I have the same needs for privacy and serenity and understanding as any other mother-to-be. I don't know where else to turn." Alex turned away, stifling another sob.

He was irresistible—massive, grotesque, ugly as the hind end of a dachshund perhaps, but irresistible. The sympathetic onlookers and eavesdroppers found themselves moved by this big . . . person's . . . courage and candor. Naomi felt herself softening like butter left out on a radiator. She took Alexandra's huge hands into hers.

"Alexandra, you've come to the right place," she said throatily. "And you know something else?"

"No, what?" asked Alex.

Naomi beamed at him, blinking back tears.

"You are beautiful. Yes, you are."

"You are beautiful," the staffers echoed.

Naomi looked at Larry with heartfelt, albeit New Age, emotion. "Larry, share with us?"

The little guy cleared his throat. "You are beautiful," he said to Alex, choking a little on the words.

Naomi leaned forward to embrace Alex, although her arms didn't quite reach around him and his belly bumped against her awkwardly. Everybody uttered that *awwwww* that people murmur at Benji the Dog movies, and Alex sighed in relief. The worst appeared to be over.

"Willow?" Naomi beckoned to a staff member. "Show Alexandra to her room." Alex and Larry followed the staff member up the main stairway and down the second-floor corridor to the room.

"I'm catching a flight to Vancouver tomorrow," Larry said briskly. "The meetings with Lyndon Pharmaceutical shouldn't take more than three or four days."

Willow unlocked the room door, and they followed her in. It was a private room, of course. The thought of Alex sharing with another pregnant roommate made Larry's few remaining hairs stand up. Willow laid Alex's overnight case on the bed and called their attention to the room's amenities. "Temperature control . . . call button . . .

extra blankets . . ." Larry pulled a twenty dollar bill out of his wallet and offered it to the young woman.

"See that she's taken care of, will you, Willow?"

"Of course," smiled the girl, waving the tip away. She left, closing the door behind her. Exhausted from the wearying charade, Alex slumped down to a sitting position on the bed. Larry looked around Alex's new home, which was bright and spacious, with wide windows overlooking the gardens, and pretty-pretty colored prints hanging on the walls. The colors and the furniture had been carefully chosen for their maximum soothing effect; it was like being in a room-sized womb.

"Nice, huh?" said Larry approvingly.

Alex didn't answer, but instead he looked soberly at Larry. "Larry? Do you really think the baby's going to be born?" he asked quietly, expressing at last his deepest fear.

Larry Arbogast considered the question. It deserved a completely truthful answer, and he gave it. "I want to say 'of course,'" he said slowly. "But there's no precedent for this. The fetus is already crowding your liver and intestines. Vital arteries are compromised. Am I concerned? Sure!"

"But everything will be all right?" Alex pressed him anxiously.

Larry grinned suddenly. "It better be. It's my kid, too, you know."

Alex returned the smile with a hesitant one of his own. He felt better now. "Thanks . . . for everything," he said softly.

"You take care," Larry answered gruffly. He held his arms out to Alex, who lumbered clumsily up from the bed and embraced him. It was an awkward hug, given the vast difference in their sizes and the intrusive bulk of Junior. But what it lacked in grace it made up for in sincerity. They were friends now, real friends.

Then Larry left, and Alex was alone. He went to the window and watched Larry drive away. Then he sat quietly by the window, just looking out. He saw the sun reflecting off a goldfish pond, saw a group of pregnant women in a circle on the lawn, taking a class in pregnancy yoga. Everything was calm; everything was tranquil.

Everything except Alex's mind, which was in turmoil. He stood up and took off the wig, which was making his head sweat. Then he went to the telephone and dialed Diana's number at the laboratory. It rang and rang, and then the answering machine picked up the call, and he heard Diana's taped voice, asking the caller to leave a message.

"Diana, it's Alex," he said. "If you're there, please pick up. I need to talk to you." He felt the sudden conviction that Diana was right there, monitoring the call, and he wasn't wrong. What he didn't picture were the tears that glistened in her eyes.

"Please call me," he continued. "I know you're mad and upset, and you have every right to be, but we still have to deal with this . . ."

But Diana did not call back. So Alex got through the next couple of days somehow, doing yoga exercises, chafed and sweating under his wig and his disguising caftan garments, taking breathing exercises and rest periods in which Gregorian chants were piped in over the public address system, and calling, calling Diana every chance he got. As soon as he was alone in his room, Alex would pick up the receiver and punch in Diana's number, only to meet the unyielding answering machine again and again.

"Please, I wish you would call me. You and your Junior have made me happier than I ever thought I could be. Please give me a chance to share it with you."

No answer. No call back.

"Please, *please* call me. I'm going to sleep now . . . My number is . . . Oh, I've left it ten times already. Please, call me, *please*? Good night, Diana."

He hung up the phone, disconsolate, then, on a sudden impulse, he picked the receiver up and kissed it. He hung up again, and settled down to sleep, trying to find a comfortable position for Junior. He couldn't sleep on his stomach anymore, and it was hard for him to breathe lying on his back; at last, worn out, he managed to find a position lying on his side, curled up like the fetus he was carrying, and dropped off.

The following day, all the mothers-to-be gathered on the south lawn of Casitas Madres, sitting in a circle for another of their uplifting sessions with Naomi. Wearing one of his concealing caftans, his wig firmly in place, his makeup and earrings on, Alex was among their number. Naomi Bender went from one to another, handing out pens and pieces of paper cut in the shape of leaves.

"The leaf—the symbol of spring, of rebirth," she told the attentive circle, "and renewal. On one side, I want you to write down your biggest fear as a mother-to-be, and on the other side, the empowerment which enables you to overcome that fear. No names, this isn't a test."

Alex sat quietly for a moment, just staring at his leaf and thinking. Then he began to scribble. When the anonymous leaves were all written and collected, Naomi began to read them aloud. "My biggest fear is that I'm not exactly what you would call a natural mother. How will I ever cope?"

Alex looked away, but listened intently, because it was Alex's own leaf Naomi was reading. "Well," she said brightly, "I think we've *all* had *that* feeling at one time or another." The group laughed gently, and a ripple of murmured assent passed among them. Only Alex sat silent, inspecting a flower.

Naomi turned the leaf over, and a small frown puckered her brow. "Her solution is . . . blank. She left it blank." She looked around the group, which was emitting rumbles of concern, and looked especially hard at Alexandra, who seemed to be avoiding her eyes. Naomi had a suspicion that it was Alexandra who had despaired of a solution. That big woman needed a little therapy to change that defeatist attitude, starting now.

"Let's dispense right now with the myth that some are born with the maternal instinct and some are not," Naomi stated firmly. "The little girl who tends her doll collection is no more a born mother than the tomboy who lives next door. There is no standard, there are no 'naturals'"

Alex sighed; he hoped that Naomi's words were true, because as much as he looked forward to Junior's birth, he dreaded it. He felt so alone. He glanced across the lawn to the main house and sat up straight with a gasp of surprise. Diana Reddin was there, at the door of the house, being shown to a seat on the front patio by one of the attendants. She was wearing a soft jersey suit of dark green, with a string of pearls around her neck, and she looked absolutely wonderful.

"There is only the individual," continued Naomi, "doing her personal best to love her child uncondition-

149

ally, and to receive that love in return. And we're *all* born seeking to love and be loved."

But Alex was no longer listening to Naomi. She had lost his attention. He was up on his feet and moving along the path toward Diana, his face wreathed in smiles. Seeing him coming, she too stood up and began to walk, meeting him halfway.

"Very fetching," Diana said, eying Alex's costume and wig. She raised one eyebrow in gentle mockery. "You might want to rethink the earrings, though."

But Alex wasn't aware of how grotesque he looked to her; he was so happy to see Diana that her barbs didn't even prick him. "I'm glad you came," he told her warmly. "I was starting to wonder if I'd ever hear from you."

"I needed some time to think," Diana said seriously, the mocking smile leaving her face.

"And?" Alex asked, holding his breath. There was an eternity of suspense in that single syllable.

"It's really unfair what you've done. Monumentally unfair," she said angrily.

Alex nodded; he agreed with her totally. "Can you forgive me?"

"If I were you, I wouldn't be asking *anything* of me."

Even under the grotesque mask of makeup, one could see the disappointment in Alex's face. "Okay. Look, I would understand if you never wanted to see me again. And I take full responsibility for the baby."

But Diana was shaking her head vigorously. "No such luck, you big jerk. Let's get a few things straight. Junior's mine, too. Don't you ever forget that."

"I won't," said Alex, smiling.

"*I'm* the mother, *you're* the father. You got that?!"

150

Diana's expression was serious, there was a glint in her eye, and her tone of voice was definitely a *get-things-straight* one.

Despite all that, Alex's smile became a grin. "Yes."

"We're going to work out an intelligent way to share these responsibilities."

"Yes," agreed Alex happily.

"The care, the nurturing, the sense of family."

"Yes, yes, yes!"

Diana waved one hand at Alex's swollen belly. "This little . . . mix-up . . . here . . . stays our secret. I hope you weren't planning to capitalize on your experiment. I won't have my child burdened with that." Her lips set firmly together. "Won't have it."

Alex nodded his head. "No, me also. But Banes wants to. He's dangerous."

Diana understood. "Yes, but it's only a couple more weeks. We've managed up until now . . . *you've* managed," she conceded grudgingly. "How are you feeling?"

"Better for seeing you again," said Alex with a smile.

Diana couldn't help it; she had to return his smile at last, relaxing her guard. Things were okay between them again, and Alex Hesse had never been happier in his life.

They strolled through the grounds of Casitas Madres like a pair of old friends, and though Alex longed to touch Diana, even just her hand, he didn't dare. He knew he was conspicuous enough already. They wound up on the front patio of the main house, sitting down to tall lemon-rimmed glasses of ice tea at one of the small bistro tables.

"They made wonderful iced tea here," Alex said.

"Yes," Diana agreed, taking a long sip. "It's *very* good."

"Kind of minty."

They were sitting side by side, drinking the refreshing tea, when suddenly Diana asked, "Do you have a private room?"

"Yes. Why?"

"We have some business to attend to, I think," she said in her crisp British way.

"What business?"

Diana leaned over the table and looked him right in the eye. He blinked, but she did not. "Call me old-fashioned, but I'll be damned if I'm having a kid with a man I've never slept with." Diana stood up and held her hands out to him. "Well? Are you coming?"

Suddenly Alex didn't care how conspicuous he looked to anybody. He took her hand, got to his feet, and almost not daring to believe how happy he was, he took Diana Reddin—the mother of the child he was carrying—up the stairs to his private room.

What passed between them there is none of our business, and happened behind a locked door. But rest assured that it was loving, beautiful, deep, fulfilling, and left a thoroughly satisfied Alex Hesse snoring on his back with a huge gap-toothed grin on his face.

Diana was wide awake, sitting at Alex's dressing table, staring at her face in the mirror. No woman had ever been involved in a relationship like this. There were no precedents; no expert advice articles in *Cosmo* or any other of the glossy women's magazines; no girlfriend she could confide in. What she had was a situation unique in the annals of medical history, not to mention the annals of love.

Because this *was* love. If she hadn't been convinced of that before she went to bed with Alex, Diana was convinced of it now. She had never before felt such a closeness to another human being. That tenderness and passion she had always been afraid she would never experience—because she would never find the man she thought of as "Mr. Right"—she had just been dispensing and receiving so lavishly her head was still spinning.

And Junior, *her* Junior, was almost a reality. Diana could feel the baby moving and kicking inside Alex, and it was as though she were carrying the child herself. She understood fully now the strange and mysterious connection to Alex she had been feeling. Without knowing it—for how could Diana possibly have guessed it?—she had been drawn to her own egg, her own embryo, her own fetus, her own baby, developing inside of Alex.

She loved Alex, but she couldn't separate that love from the love she had for Junior. Nor did she have to; that was the best part of all. She could have them both. They would all be a family.

Diana had indeed been *very* angry when Alex told her about Junior. She'd felt cheated and deceived. But now she only marveled at the strange tricks destiny played when you weren't looking. How could she possibly have known that Alexander Hesse would turn out to be the very man she would have chosen to be her Junior's father! Strong, smart, sensitive. Sexy. Well, technically, perhaps Alex was more mother than father, but they would sort all that out later, Diana told herself with her customary practical common sense. It was all going to turn out well. She was in love, she was loved, she was going to be a parent, and who could have predicted that everything would come to her all at once? And arrive in the grotesque form of a man in a dreadful wig and caftan?

Diana stood up and finished dressing quickly, while Alex lay sleeping on. She smoothed her hose, slipped into her pumps, and picked up her string of pearls, intending to fasten them around her neck. Then, in a burst of affection, she had another idea. Tiptoeing over to the bed, she leaned forward, gazing into Alex's happy, sleeping face, and placed the pearls in his hand, gently bending his fingers around them. Then she kissed his bulging belly softly, whispering bye-bye to Junior, and she tiptoed out of the room.

In Vancouver, Larry Arbogast was enjoying satisfaction as well. He had been as successful at winning Lyndon Pharmaceuticals as Alex had been at winning Diana. He sat now in the well-appointed mahogany-paneled boardroom of the megalithic corporation, looking out at the unfamiliar skyline of Vancouver and humming to himself. One of Lyndon's lawyers interrupted Larry's reverie by placing a large stack of documents down in front of him on the polished burl of the rare African wood conference table.

"If everything is satisfactory, please sign all eight copies where they're tagged . . ."

Ten minutes later, Larry was happily signing. He looked up. "And once we have European approval, the FDA will fall in line for testing in the States?"

The Lyndon executive nodded with every confidence. "Leave it to us."

Breakfast at Casitas Madres was always a cheery, communal affair. Long trestle tables were set out with every kind of healthy food—sliced oranges and kiwis, hefty chunks of melon, heaping bowls of granola, whole-grain bread, big muffins dotted with fruit and nuts, low-fat milk, cholesterol-free omelets made with egg white only. Breakfast was a buffet meal at which the pregnant ladies renewed themselves spiritually every morning, while they stuffed their faces.

Normally, Ms. Alexandra Hesse would have been pitching right into the food, consuming vast quantities of vitamins and minerals for Junior. But this morning Alex was feeling rather unwell. He fidgeted in his chair while his backache and belly cramps grew steadily worse, until the pains had become so bad he couldn't sit any longer. Unsteadily, he rose to his feet and, grimacing with pain, walked slowly out of the dining room and up the stairs, two feet on every step, until he got to his room, where he locked his door and collapsed on his bed, writhing in agony.

Something was wrong, terribly wrong. The pain was excruciating. Junior wanted out, and there was no way out. Alex realized with a cry of dismay that he was going into labor. He was miles away from anyone who could help him, alone, helpless, and in labor. And Larry, his doctor, his best friend, was in Canada. Another long groan, half pain, half fear, escaped Alex's wretched lips.

The telephone rang. With a great effort, Alex picked up the receiver. On the other end, he could hear Larry Arbogast's jubilant voice. Thank Heaven!

"Alex? We've got it!! Lyndon's coming in as partners and pushing us to the FDA!"

A low groan from Alex.

"Alex? Are you all right?" Larry sounded suddenly alarmed. Curled up on the bed, rocking from side to side in anguish, Alex could only say, "Larry . . . please . . . hurry."

You didn't have to tell him twice. Larry slammed down the phone and made it into a taxi before Alex's next contraction had trailed off. Thank God he'd left the Chrysler at the San Francisco airport, he thought. At the Vancouver airport first class lounge, in the three minutes before his flight was called, he made one credit card phone call to San Francisco, to his partner, Dr. Edwin Sneller.

"Ned? Larry. We've got an emergency c-section tonight. I want everybody out of the building except you and Louise. We're the whole team. We're gonna have to wing it. Gotta go. I'm flying in, be there in a few hours. No, I'll explain later. Just do it!" When he hung up, Larry walked nervously down the ramp to the waiting plane. God, he hoped he could trust Ned Sneller! The Fertility Center had to be stone empty for Alex's cesarean section; if the story got out, there would be hell to pay.

All the way back from Vancouver to San Francisco, Larry sat staring out the aircraft window, seeing nothing of the scenery below. He was thinking hard about Alex and Junior, and he was really worrying. It was Larry Arbogast who'd gotten Alex into this mess; it had all been his own idea, and now the big guy was suffering. Alex's life was in danger. Junior's life was in danger. Oddly enough, when you consider it was Larry Arbogast doing the worrying, he didn't spare a single thought for the very lucrative pharmaceutical contracts sitting next to him in his briefcase.

All Larry could think about was that, at this very moment, while he was still miles away, his best friend Alex Hesse was in great pain. He might be losing his baby. He might even be dying.

Chapter Nine

He's Having My Baby

After breakfast at Casitas Madres, Alexandra Hesse had turned up missing. Naomi sent out a few of her trusted employees to look for her. She was worried about Alexandra; the woman seemed moody and depressed, and although she tried to fit in, she often seemed alien to the loving, nurturing environment they all worked so hard to foster here. But the attendants came back empty-handed. They couldn't find her anywhere.

Alexandra wasn't in the pottery workshop or the sensitivity workshop or sitting in on the mothering class. She wasn't at the La Leche League lecture, the yoga class, or in the lowest-impact aerobics group. They peeped into the music lounge, but Alexandra wasn't in there listening to the sounds of the rain forest, nor was she walking through the Contemplation Arbor or raking sand in the Zen Garden or sitting and meditating by the goldfish pond. They looked for her in the herbarium, thinking that she might be enjoying a little self-aromatherapy, but she wasn't. Where was Ms. Alexandra Hess?

By ten-fifteen the staff was starting to worry. Nobody had seen her for over two hours, and Alexandra was one hard-to-miss lady. After a second brief search, a couple of attendants discovered that Alexandra's door wouldn't open, and found her at last, barricaded in her locked room, refusing to come out.

This was a no-no. Locked doors were not allowed. All the mothers-to-be at Casitas Madres had to be where they could be supervised at every moment. One never knew when a pregnancy could turn into a miscarriage or labor. The rules set down by the insurance company were very clear. No locked doors.

Within minutes, a crowd had gathered outside the door, banging on it for admission. But Alex had no intention of letting anybody into his room. He lay writhing and moaning on his bed, hurting so bad he could barely stand it, his fingers shaking as he dialed the number of Diana's laboratory. When she answered, all he could gasp out was, "Hurry, Diana, I need you . . ."

Without even stopping to hang up the phone, Diana grabbed up her car keys and hotfooted it out of the lab, Jenny and Arthur, Alice, Minnie and Moe, and the chimp baby Michelle all staring after her in bewilderment.

"Alexandra! Please! Open the door!" pleaded Naomi. Obviously something was very wrong with Alexandra. Was she only down in the dumps and frightened, or was something more serious the matter with her? Could labor actually have begun? A group of pregnant women had gathered in the hallway outside, buzzing among themselves. Naomi had summoned a couple of the staff doctors, and they, too, were there, adding the weight of their knuckles to Alex's door.

"I want my Larry!" Alex called in a falsetto.

"I know that. But in the meantime, let's just have the doctors take a look at you. Come on, now . . ." said Naomi wheedlingly.

"But I don't *know* these doctors!" cried Alex, desperate. If there was one thing that mustn't happen, it was for strange doctors to examine him now.

But if Alexandra was in labor and having her baby right now, they couldn't possibly wait for Larry. The doctors had to attend to her. Every moment counted. Naomi took a set of master keys out of her pocket. "They're *fine* doctors," she called encouragingly. "You can trust them. We're coming in now . . ." And she turned the key in the lock.

The lock opened, but the door held fast, blocked by the heavy dresser that Alex had painfully pushed against it.

"Alexandra! You're being completely irrational!" yelled Naomi, now getting really annoyed.

On the Pacific Coast Highway, Larry Arbogast was speeding around treacherous curves, his foot on the gas, his eyes fixed firmly on the road.

Behind him by less than ten or so miles, although neither was aware of it, came Diana Reddin. She was driving on sheer instinct, because her mind was not on the winding road under her wheels, but on Alex and on Junior. Would they be all right? They *must* be all right! she thought with desperation. Everything good in her life was tied up in that one package, and now that package was in terrible pain, moaning and whimpering and begging her to hurry. *Hold on, Alex darling. Hold on, Junior, baby. I'm coming as fast as I can.*

Larry skidded to a noisy stop outside the main building of Casitas Madres and hit the ground running. He dashed past the protesting receptionist and made for the stairs. Above him on the landing he could hear pounding and loud voices. Larry reached the landing in time to see a pair of doctors pushing hard on Alex's door, and the door was already beginning to give. Tearing down the corridor, Larry elbowed his way past all the pregnant females, nudged the doctors aside, and yelled out at the top of his lungs.

"Pumpkin?!"

"Larry?"

"Everything's gonna be okay!"

The door swung open. Alex/Alexandra stood there swaying, grimacing, and clutching his/her belly tightly. He was pale, and there were fine beads of sweat on his brows and upper lip. "Something's wrong with Junior," he said pathetically. He was in a great deal of pain, yet his concern was not for himself, but for the baby.

Larry shook his head. "Junior's going to be fine." Still, he recognized labor when he saw it and he knew with an obstetrician's certainty that there wasn't a minute to waste. He grabbed the wheelchair that was waiting out in the hall, swung it around, and popped Alex into it. They took off at a run down the corridor, with the pregnant women waving and yelling encouragement.

"Good luck!"

"Don't forget to breathe!"

Breathe. Good idea. A very frightened, wide-eyed Alex Hesse began his Lamaze panting.

Just as Larry and Alex were leaving Casitas Madres by the front door, Diana's car drew up and she came dashing out. She spotted Alex sitting in a wheelchair, being pushed by Larry Arbogast, his face contorted in pain, while behind them came a buzzing stream of attendants and a group of women with very big bellies.

Rushing over to Larry's Chrysler, Diana demanded frantically, "Is he all right?"

"What are you doing here?" Larry asked crossly, as he stowed the panting Alex into the back seat.

"Where else would I be?" yelled Diana, equally cross. "It's my baby!" A collective gasp, followed by a curious murmur, ran through the eavesdropping crowd.

"It's my baby, too! Don't try to shut me out!" argued Larry.

"Stop it. Let's go!" Alex's roar came through teeth gritted in pain, but in his normal man's voice.

This sent another flutter of consternation through the ranks of the onlookers. The crowd oohed and aahed again. Things were getting more mysteriously exciting by the minute.

Larry jumped behind the wheel, and Diana got into the passenger seat next to him. Larry stepped on the gas, and they sped off north, leaving behind them one very confused bunch of patients and attendants at Casitas Madres. They would be racking their brains and talking about today for a long, long time to come.

Noah Banes was frustrated and furious. Larry Arbogast and Alex Hesse had vanished off the edge of the world. Nobody had seen them; none of his spies on campus could tell him where they were. He had paid people watching The Fertility Center, but Dr. Arbogast hadn't been there in days. And time was growing very short. Banes was afraid that the two of them had gone off to some exotic place to have the baby, like Barbados or Detroit, some place where he couldn't follow. That would effectively put the kibosh on Banes's plans and Banes's ambitions. Arbogast and Hesse could come back, with or without the baby, and nobody would ever know the truth.

Noah Banes's office telephone rang. On the other end was one of the custodians at The Fertility Center.

"Mr. Banes? It's Pete Clifton at the medical center. You said to let you know when something was up here. Well, something's definitely up. They're sending everybody home and there's something about an emergency Caesar . . . Caesar something. That mean anything to you?"

Did that mean anything? *Did* it! Suddenly, bells began to ring melodiously in Banes's ears, celestial curtains parted, and his enraptured eyes beheld the gates of Heaven opening wide. "More than you could ever understand," he said buoyantly. Now *there* was a fifty-dollar tip well spent. "Thanks."

Hanging up the phone, Noah Banes bellowed for his assistant. "Samantha! It's showtime! Call down our media list and tell them to meet me in front of Arbogast's offices!" An inspiration struck him, and he added, "President Sawyer, too!" Yes, the president of the university should definitely be there when history was being made.

Banes ran it down in his head. Alex Hesse was ready to pop. Larry Arbogast was going to do a top-secret cesarean section, and the first baby ever carried by a male was going to be born not in Barbados or Detroit but right here in San Francisco. The two of them thought they could cut him, Noah Banes, out of the loop. They thought they could carry off the first male childbirth in history without the presence of the media or the university. Well, think again, bozos. Noah Banes's mama didn't raise no stupid children.

He was going to be there when the baby was born. The president of the university was going to be there when the baby was born. The cameras, photographers, reporters, and *Hard Copy* were going to be there when the baby was born. This would be the biggest media event since . . . since . . . No, the biggest media event *ever*. For the first time in history the headlines in the supermarket tabloids would be telling the truth. Banes could see those headlines now: "MAN HAS BABY." "BYE-BYE MOMMY, DADDY GOES IT ALONE."

Noah Banes was exultant; he did a little dance for sheer joy. He could smell promotion, honors, a larger office, a bigger staff, a lot more money. Maybe even a book contract, a film deal. Movie of the week. Leland University would get a large chunk of the glory, but some of the shine would rub off on him, Noah Banes. Oh, they'll thank me for this, Banes thought and chuckled to himself. They *will* thank me.

The Chrysler careened around a hairpin turn. In the back seat, Alex was whipped from one side of the car to the other, and he groaned out loud.

"Do we have to go around so many curves?" demanded Diana nervously. It was painful for her to see Alex in such great physical distress.

"Just a couple more miles of this," Larry answered mildly, with surprising patience. "How're you doing, Alex?"

"I think Junior kicked a hole in something," Alex gasped. He resumed his Lamaze panting.

Larry reached for the car phone and punched in The Fertility Center's center. "Louise? Gimme Ned Sneller. Hang on, Alex."

"I want to die," groaned Alex, and Diana turned around in the front seat to face him. "Breathe, breathe . . . ," she told him urgently, panting in his face to set him an example.

Ned Sneller's voice came over the cellular phone, amplified by the speakerphone in his office. "Larry?"

"Ned, we're about a half hour away."

"Larry, you want to tell me what's going on? Somebody from the university's got a bunch of media waiting out front."

Media! Larry slammed his fist down on the dashboard. "Banes! Damn. Can you get rid of them?"

"I don't think so," Sneller said. "They seem to be pretty well encamped. What *is* this?"

"It's . . . it's . . . I don't want to discuss this on cellular. Meet me out front." Larry hit the Off button and put the phone back in its cradle. He was definitely worried now.

This was disastrous news, the worst possible. With every minute that passed making a big difference, The Fertility Center, ready for Alex's delivery, looked now as though it were off limits. How could they even get inside to the operating room, with the press people hanging around the front door like circling vultures?

There was no way that Larry was going to subject his pal Alex to a media circus on his way to the operating table. It would be the end of all their plans and hopes. He could see it now. There would be screaming headlines in all the cheap tabloids, the exploitation on TV talk shows, the mockery, the snide jokes by Leno and Letterman— no, Larry couldn't let that happen.

Yet The Fertility Center was their only possibility. It was the only hospital that would afford them a safe haven, with the privacy needed for the delivery, not to mention that it was the only hospital at which Dr. Lawrence Arbogast was accredited to perform surgery.

"What are we going to do?" Alex groaned.

"I'm thinking, I'm thinking . . ." Larry cudgeled his brains. "We need . . ."

"A diversion!" finished Diana.

"There's no *time!*" moaned Alex. "Oooowwww!"

But Diana was right. A diversion was *exactly* what they needed, and Larry would have to improvise, and fast. His face brightened as he had a sudden inspiration. "Hang on . . . ," he yelled, putting his foot down on the accelerator.

"This *better* be big, Banes," said Edward Sawyer sternly. "You called me away from dinner with the university's single largest benefactor."

The distinguished-looking president of Leland University stood huddled with Noah Banes outside The Fertility Center. Gathered around the front door was a knot of reporters and video cameras, ready and waiting for the arrival of the big story, whatever it was. So far, Banes had been keeping them all in the dark.

"Oh, it's big, Edward," Banes said with confidence. "Literally and figuratively."

Banes stepped forward and beckoned the media. When he was satisfied that he had captured their attention, satisfied that the minicams were trained on him and film was rolling, he began his announcement. In his most sonorous voice, he said importantly, "Ladies and gentlemen, thank you for coming. I am Noah Banes, director of Leland University's Lufkin Biotechnology Research Center, and this is Edward Sawyer, president of Leland University."

Sawyer waved benevolently to the cameras. His very presence was lending credence to the story, whatever it was that was about to happen here.

"It is our great thrill and profound honor," Banes continued pompously, "to announce what is certainly the most momentous breakthrough in medical science in our time." Banes paused for effect, and then he delivered his bombshell. "Dr. Alexander Hesse of my staff will be arriving here shortly to undergo procedures to deliver the baby he has, himself, carried to term."

The surprise announcement caused immediate pandemonium among the members of the media. Had they heard him right? Was a man actually going to have a baby? Who the hell was Dr. Alexander Hesse? Would the university let the minicams into the delivery room? The reporters began to surge forward, all shouting questions at once, but the question was roughly the same one: "You're saying he's pregnant?"

"That's right," Banes said, smiling broadly. What a great moment this was! "Perfect timing! Here he is now."

At that very moment, as though on cue, Larry Arbogast's car came screeching along the entrance driveway and pulled up in front of his clinic. The Chrysler braked to a sharp stop and tooted its horn. At once Dr. Edwin Sneller was seen rushing out of The Fertility Center's main entrance, pushing an empty wheelchair.

"Here we go!" yelled Larry. He flung the driver's door open and climbed out of the car. He was wearing his game face; nothing showed. Immediately the reporters and minicams converged on him, yelling their questions, shoving microphones and flashbulbs into his face.

"Easy, fellows, will you? Gimme a little room here, please? Don't crowd. My patient needs air."

Skillfully, Larry fended off the microphones as he opened the back door of the car. Instantly the cameras swung around to the back seat. A beaming Noah Banes edged forward so that he would have a place on the historic videotape.

"Where is he?!" yelled one reporter.

"Do you think this is the wave of the future?" yelled another.

"Is what?" asked Larry, all innocence.

"Men bearing children."

"What are you talking about?" asked Larry. He reached into the back seat and handed out his patient, who emerged with a pained face, doing natural childbirth panting. The patient was . . . Angela Arbogast.

"Look, honey, we're on TV," said Larry, with a grin.

Angela stopped moaning long enough to smile into the camera. "Hi, Mom." Then another contraction seized her and she let out a sharp yip.

"It's just a woman!" yelled the disappointed reporters. "Only a woman!"

Tenderly, Larry and Ned Sneller helped Angela into the wheelchair. "Hey, that's my wife you're talking about!" said Larry reproachfully.

Noah Banes reeled backward as though from a sharp body blow. He could barely catch his breath. This couldn't be happening, not to him! This was supposed to be the most significant event in twentieth-century medical history, not a debacle! What was the meretricious duo up to now? How dared they do this? Where was the pregnant Alex Hesse?

The reporters turned on Banes, furious now instead of curious. They'd been promised a lead story and had gotten a big fat nothing. "We were told there was a pregnant *man*!" they yelled at him accusingly, turning off the minicams so they wouldn't waste any more footage.

"There is!" cried Banes. "Where is he?!" he yelled desperately at Larry.

Angela doubled over very convincingly. "Oh, Larry!!" she cried out. Larry grabbed the wheelchair's handles and began to push the chair through the reporters. "Excuse us . . . coming through . . ." Dr. Sneller followed.

The reporters began to disperse, really pissed off. There was no story here. They'd all double-timed it down here on a damn wild goose chase, because Noah Banes had promised them the best story they'd ever covered. And it had turned out to be nothing . . . nothing but a pretty little woman about to give birth in a totally conventional way, in her obstetrician husband's own clinic. Big deal.

But Banes wasn't giving up yet. He tried to block the media from leaving as he yelled angrily at Larry, his face turning a color very close to purple.

"Where is he?!"

Larry let go of the wheelchair and stepped up to Banes, really close. "Banes, I've got good news and bad news. The bad news: there is no pregnant man. The good news: there's a dark cloud on your horizon." Then he grabbed Angela's wheelchair again and rushed on, cackling gleefully.

"Noah?"

At the familiar voice, Banes turned, frantic. Larry was right. There *was* a dark cloud on his horizon, and its name was Edward Sawyer. President Sawyer was standing right behind him, his lips in a thin line, his eyes glinting in fury, his face carved from stone. He was so deeply angry he was finding it difficult to speak. This unspeakable media fiasco was a humiliating experience that he and Leland University did not intend to take lightly.

Now, Noah Banes was an intelligent and practical man. He had not climbed to his present eminence by behaving rashly or placing his university president in the position of looking foolish. What he knew he should do was this: he should hang on to his cool, mollify Edward Sawyer until he could get him alone, and then calmly, dispassionately, lay out every scrap of evidence before him; the stolen Expectane samples, Alex Hesse's changing shape and mood swings, overheard conversations, and the rest of the dossier Banes had compiled. Surely, Edward would then understand and see things Banes's way. That is what Banes knew he ought to do.

What Noah Banes actually did was go to pieces, totally blowing his cool and beginning to babble frantically. "He's having a baby! I swear!" he shrieked.

"You're fired," said President Sawyer, turning his back and walking coldly away.

By now you are no doubt wandering what happened to our hero, Dr. Alexander Hesse, and why he wasn't in Larry's car. Where is he? How is he? How is Junior? What the hell is going on?

The explanation is simple: Larry Arbogast's brilliant idea for creating the perfect diversion and foiling Noah Banes was to go to Angela's house and get Angela. Angela Arbogast, by now a full nine months pregnant, was the perfect prop for getting past the press. All Larry asked her to do was pretend to be in labor and lend Diana and Alex her Mercedes.

So as the Chrysler was pulling up to the front entrance of The Fertility Center, the red Mercedes was pulling up to the rear fire escape, and Diana was scrambling out and easing the pain-wracked Alex from the passenger seat. The contractions were getting worse, and much closer together now.

Now, you know this isn't going to be easy. You know the back entrance is going to be locked tight, and all the custodians have been sent home. You know that Diana and Alex are going to have to drag themselves up the narrow ladder to the outside fire escape steps, and all the while Alex Hesse will be suffering excruciating contractions. But you have to picture a slender Diana Reddin, who played field hockey for her school, Roedean, and who was really quite strong for her size and weight but no real match for the size and weight of a heavily pregnant Alex, making her way along behind him, her hands firmly on his ass, pushing and shoving him up the ladder that led to the fire escape itself. It's quite a picture.

"It hurts so much . . . ," moaned Alex.

Diana tried psychology; anything to help, even positive imaging. "Imagine a . . . tranquil blue sea . . . sun shining . . . ," she panted, nearly out of breath with the effort of moving Alex up the ladder, ". . . birdies singing . . . cheep cheep—"

"Just push, okay?" snapped Alex.

Oh, and one more thing, before we forget. Angela was supposed to pretend she was in labor, to fool the media, right? But something Larry didn't know was that Angela actually *was* in labor. Labor had begun while she was in the Chrysler, on the way to The Fertility Center. Her contractions were still about four minutes apart, but her cervix was rapidly dilating, and the pain was spreading in rhythmic waves from her belly to her back. Her little body was getting readier by the minute to deliver a child. She doubled over in the wheelchair, huffing and puffing as she'd learned in Lamaze class.

But Larry Arbogast was not paying attention to her. He was only concentrating on getting to Alex. He and Sneller got into the elevator with the wheelchair, and Larry pressed the button for the second floor.

"Why are we stopping at two?" asked Sneller. Only offices and examining rooms were on two.

"It's a surprise."

When the elevator door opened on the second floor, Louise was waiting for them.

"Are they here?" Larry asked as he wheeled Angela out.

Louise shook her head. "Not yet."

Ned Sneller was totally confused. Was who here? Why were they on the second floor when the operating room was on the third floor? Why were they doing a c-section when Angela was obviously laboring normally? Why all the secrecy?

"Why is it just you and me, Larry? A cesarean, we really ought to have—"

"Just trust me on this, okay?" Larry wheeled Angela over to the waiting area, which was furnished like a living room, and helped her out of the wheelchair and onto a couch. Angela moaned in pain as another contraction hit her hard.

"You can quit now, Angela, we're alone," said Larry, who hadn't caught on yet.

And before she could tell him—

"Larry?!" It was Alex's voice, coming from Larry's second-floor office.

"Come on, Ned," urged Larry. "Hurry." He rushed the empty wheelchair toward his office, with Ned behind him, now completely mystified. Angela was obviously well into labor, but Larry didn't seem to be paying her any mind.

"You want to tell me what's going on?" demanded Ned, trailing Larry into his office. Once he was inside, his mouth dropped open and he gaped in astonishment.

Alex Hesse was wedged in the open fire escape window, half in and half out. He was completely stuck, like Winnie the Pooh in Rabbit's house. Behind him, out on the fire escape, somebody was evidently trying to push Alex through the window, to judge from the grunts and the huffing Ned could hear out there.

"Larry?!" wailed the anguished Alex.

"Okay, big guy, almost there." Larry grabbed one of Alex's arms and gestured with his head for Ned to grab the other. The two of them pulled hard while Diana struggled out on the fire escape, still pushing.

"On, three!" Larry yelled and nodded to Sneller. "One, two . . . *three!*"

Diana pushed and pushed, and Ned and Larry pulled and pulled, and thanks to their combined efforts, Alex suddenly popped free, like the cork from a bottle of chianti, and landed inside the office like a big, gasping fish. With Larry's help, Alex struggled to his feet and into the wheelchair. Diana climbed in the window.

Ned shook his head. Alex was huge, grotesque! There could be no possible explanation for this. "What's wrong with him?" he asked Larry.

"My best guess is that his baby's entangled in the large intestine."

His baby? *His* baby? HIS baby? "*His* baby?" gasped Ned. He took a long, hard look at Alex, taking in the pains, the huge abdomen, the look of agony on the big man's face. "Oh . . . my . . . god!"

"Wait'll you see," Larry said cheerfully, wheeling Alex to the elevator. "It's the size of a Buick."

Chapter Ten

Delivery First Class

It was bedlam inside The Fertility Center. They all piled at once into the elevator—Larry pushing Alex in the wheelchair; a white-faced Alex contorted into a puffing pretzel by the powerful contractions racking him, his features distorted by agony and Lamaze breathing; Louise; a shell-shocked Ned Sneller; and Angela, who was by now—although nobody recognized it but Angela herself and Ned Sneller, who still thought that she was the logical patient—in heavy, active labor and leaning on a worried Diana Reddin.

The operating room was ready, and it took but a few moments for Louise to prep Alex, while Larry and Ned made themselves sterile and got dressed in their surgical gowns and masks. When Alex was prepped and ready on the gurney, lying under a white sheet draped over him, which made him look like Moby Dick the Great White Whale, Larry and Ned rolled him hastily toward the operating theater.

"Not a word about this," Larry said strongly to Ned, "not to anyone, ever. Or we can kiss this place good-bye."

"Never, never," swore Ned, still in shock.

The two doctors and Louise disappeared behind the

swinging doors, leaving Angela and Diana to wait outside the operating room.

"Oh, God!" Diana prayed fervently, staring at the operating room doors. "I hope he's all right." Her entire future was behind that door, her future and everything in her present that she loved. She wished with all her heart that she could be in there with him.

Angela braced herself against a wall as a strong contraction washed over her like a tidal wave. "Huu-uuuuuuuuuuunnnhhhhh!" she groaned.

Diana turned at the sound, and her eyes widened as she realized what was happening to Angela. "You, too?"

Caught up in the contraction and too much in pain to speak, Angela could only nod her head vigorously. She waved her hand at a couch in the reception area, and a sympathetic Diana helped her reach it and supported her weight while Angela slowly lay down on her back.

"Should I call someone?" Diana offered.

Angela shook her head. Through clenched teeth she said, "I . . . want to . . . wait . . . for Larry. Huu-uuuuuunnnnhhhh!" She resumed her panting.

"Easy now, easy . . . ," murmured Diana. She tried positive imaging again, although it had failed miserably with Alex. "Let's imagine a . . . a lovely garden, clouds floating overhead like fluffy—"

"Let's imagine drugs," said Angela bluntly, and the two women shared a rueful laugh.

"Bad, eh?" asked Diana softly.

"You don't know . . . how . . . lucky you are," gasped Angela.

Her words struck Diana. It was true, she thought suddenly. She hadn't once stopped to think about how lucky she was. Since the dawn of time, women had been bitching and moaning about how easy men had it because women were compelled by nature to bear the babies. Women complained that no man could understand fully what motherhood was all about. But look at how lucky I am, she marveled to herself. Alex loves me and I love him, and we're going to have a wonderful life together. My Junior is his Junior, the child I always dreamed of having. And for all these months Alex has done it all; I haven't had to lift a finger. As for empathy, no man in the history of the world will ever be able to empathize with a woman . . . with me . . . like my Alex. If ever a masculine man was in touch with his feminine side, it was Alex. I am *so* lucky.

But first, before the luck would count, Alex and Junior had a dreadful ordeal ahead of them. They both had to survive the operation—delicate, unprecedented, and very dangerous. Diana pictured Alex unconscious on the operating table, and her heart trembled for him. She gave a fervent thought to Larry, and wished him godspeed, and hoped he was as good a surgeon as he claimed to be.

I promise, she told Alex silently, that *I'll* carry and deliver our next child. After all, fair's fair.

But now there was Angela to look after. "What can I do?" Diana asked gently.

"Hold my hand?" Angela whispered, and Diana took her new friend's hand and prepared to stay beside Angela through the difficult time ahead.

In the operating room, under the large, round overhead light, Alice was swabbing Alex's belly with antiseptic where the incision would be made. Alex looked up at his trusted lab assistant with surprise.

"Alice, I'm glad you're here," he whispered. Larry

must have phoned ahead; Larry must have let her in on this. Good old Larry!

"Wouldn't want to miss this, Boss," the loyal Alice whispered back.

Larry approached the head of the table, an anesthetic mask in his hand.

"Larry?" Alex looked up into his friend's round face hidden behind a green surgical mask. There was so much he wanted to say to him . . . He trusted him . . . He . . .

"You relax," Larry said gently, putting the mask over Alex's nose and mouth. "I'll take it from here. Count back from one hundred."

Alex inhaled deeply. "One hundred," he murmured. "Ninety-nine . . . nine . . . ty . . . eight . . . nine—" The last thing he saw was Larry's brown eyes looking down at him, and suddenly he knew he wasn't afraid anymore. His eyes flickered shut, and Alex Hesse entered deep anesthesia.

Larry and Ned began to work, assisted by Alice and Louise. They were so concentrated on what they were doing that the time passed very quickly.

Outside in the waiting room, time was passing very slowly. Angela's contractions were coming closer and closer together, each one washing over her little body and carrying it up in a giant tsunami of agony. This was childbirth, the natural province of the female, and with exquisite irony, it was taking place in the most up-to-date medical facility in San Francisco, but it was taking place in the time-honored, old-fashioned way—a woman laboring alone in "natural childbirth," with no painkillers, no drugs, no surgical instruments, with only another woman to comfort her.

Diana mopped Angela's sweating forehead with her handkerchief and checked her wristwatch. "Just over a minute," she told her. Her fingers ached where Angela had clutched them so tightly.

"Wish he'd hurry up," panted Angela.

But Larry couldn't hurry up. Inside the operating room, the little team of two men and two women—and Alex and Junior, of course—were making medical history. The baby had grown and developed in a place where it was not natural for a pregnancy to take place, and in doing so had usurped the space of Alex's own vital organs. The last ultrasound examination had revealed Alex's organs compromised and in danger of rupture. And, for the last several hours, the baby had been punching and kicking Alex's viscera in its desperate search for the exit. It would require enormous delicacy, fearless improvisation, and incredible surgical skill to bring both the baby and its parent out of this alive and in one piece.

At last, just when Diana thought she couldn't stand it another minute, just when she was holding herself back from dashing into the operating room, Larry emerged, the picture of exhaustion, pulling the mask off his face.

Diana stood up, trembling. Her mouth was suddenly very dry and her heart began to pound like a trip-hammer in her chest. "Larry?" she croaked.

He smiled, and his entire round face lit up like the Rockefeller Center Christmas tree when they hit the switch. "Eleven pounds, six ounces, and she's got her mother's looks. Father and daughter, doing just fine."

Tears of joy sprang to Diana's eyes, and she uttered a little cry of gladness and ran to Larry, throwing her arms around his neck.

Larry patted her back. "Go on in."

Diana gestured toward the suffering Angela. "I think you've got another delivery, Doctor," she said happily, and headed for the recovery room to see her wonderful man again and to make the acquaintance of her miraculous baby daughter.

Angela groaned and, placing one hand against the violently aching small of her back, tried to struggle to her feet.

"*Angela?!*"

Larry rushed to her side. It was true. She *was* in labor and, by the look of it, very close to delivery. He began to massage her back, speaking gently into her ear as she huffed away in her Lamaze breathing.

"Okay, okay, talk to me . . . How close?" Larry asked in his best professional manner.

"The contractions are about a minute apart." And another one hit right then, making Angela cry out and grab Larry's hand tightly.

A minute apart! She was getting ready to explode! "Easy now, easy . . . Breathe . . . breathe . . . Louise! Get me a wheelchair!" he hollered.

The contraction began to subside and then passed away. Angela slumped against his shoulder. "Why didn't you tell someone?" asked Larry.

"I wanted you."

Suddenly Larry felt a lump rising in his throat. Angela's faith in him, her complete trust, touched him very deeply. She had been willing to go through childbirth without any help, rather than ask for help from anybody else but him. He felt a great tenderness for her.

Angela was worn out; she seemed very frail. Her makeup had long ago been washed off by her perspiration, leaving her face naked and vulnerable and looking very much like a little girl's. Her hair was damp and sticking to her forehead and cheeks, and her huge eyes were larger than ever, with pain and fear. Larry experienced a sharp pang of sympathy just looking at her.

"Okay, okay, you've got me," he reassured her gently.

Angela's fingers tightened on Larry's, and she looked up into his face. "Oh, Larry, it *hurts*!" she moaned.

"Won't be long now," he promised. Then, uncomfortably, he asked her, "You want Louise to . . . call the father?"

Angela managed a feeble wry smile. "Not much point. I don't know where he is, anyway."

Larry made one more try. "So it's definitely not . . ."

Angela shook her head no. "You knew that."

"Yeah, I know," he said in a low tone. "But *he* knows, right?"

A bitter look shaded Angela's eyes, and she turned her face away. "Yeah. Sent me a dozen roses and an autographed picture of himself—" She gasped as another contraction slammed at her body. "With the *band*!"

Louise came rushing up with the wheelchair. Larry couldn't wait for the contraction to end; he had to get Angela prepped for delivery right away. Even without examining her, he could tell she was fully dilated.

"Breathe through it!" he urged. "That's it, that's it . . ." To Louise, he ordered, "Prep Number Two." He began to push the chair out of the waiting area.

"Epidural?" asked Louise, meaning the anesthetic.

Larry shook his head. "No, she wants it to be natural—"

"*Drugs!*" shrieked Angela. "*Yes!!*"

Alex was sitting up in bed in the recovery room, cradling his baby in his arms. She was swaddled in a receiving blanket. Diana stood silently in the doorway, drinking in the sight of them. Alex looked wonderful. There was color in his cheeks again, and the look of anguish that Diana couldn't bear to see was washed away without a trace. When Diana came in, he looked up from the infant's face and smiled broadly.

"We've got a baby girl," he said happily. He wriggled over to make room for Diana on the bed, and she lay down beside him, looking into the baby's face, which peeped out from the blanket in the most enchanting way.

"She's so beautiful," breathed Diana in awe. It was true; the baby, thanks to her size and weight, was absolutely blooming, with a full head of golden hair, a rosy complexion, and well-defined features. She looked not like a newborn but like a child already two or three months old. The baby looked back at Diana out of deep blue eyes that actually sparkled. Diana melted utterly, then and forever.

"Isn't she sweet?" purred Alex.

"Hello, darling," Diana cooed to the little girl.

"She has your eyes," Alex said fondly.

"And your ears, look—"

"Your legs, I hope," said Alex, opening the blanket to show Diana.

"God forbid," laughed Diana. She reached over and kissed Alex with love and passion. The baby, caught in the middle, began to whimper.

"There, there . . . ," said Diana soothingly.

"It's okay, little—" Alex said, and then stopped.

Little *what*? Diana and Alex looked at each other. They had never discussed a name for their baby. "What should we call her?" Alex asked.

And in the same instant, they both knew the answer.

"Junior?" they said at the same time.

Of course, Junior. Had there ever been any doubt? She had always been Junior. Even before conception, even before boy and girl had met and joined in the petri dish, she had been Junior. Junior the miracle baby, who had come into the world in a manner entirely unique, who had brought two people together and taught them what it meant to love, and who was born to be the nucleus of a happy nuclear family. Alex and Diana looked down at her in wonder and joy.

Angela Arbogast was in the final stage of childbirth, and events were sweeping her along like a whirlwind. Larry and Louise had managed to get her from the wheelchair to the birthing bed in Delivery Room Number Two, where she lay thrashing, groaning, and panting.

"Come on, come on—one more push!" Standing at the foot of the bed, between Angela's outstretched legs, Dr. Lawrence Arbogast, obstetrician extraordinaire, exhorted his patient. "Ready and—*Push! Push! Push!*"

"*Huuuuuuuuunnnnnnnnnnnnnnnnhhhhhhhhhhhh!*" yelled Angela, with her last ounce of strength.

And then came the most wonderful sound in the world—the first squalling cry of a healthy newborn baby. Angela uttered a sob of relief. It was over. Larry beamed from ear to ear.

"It's a boy! Angela, it's a boy!"

Her face wet with tears, Angela held her arms out for her son.

"Okay, little guy." Larry cradled him tenderly as he brought him around the bed to his mother, "Yes, yes, there we go . . ." He laid the infant down gently in Angela's arms and sat down close beside her. Both of them gazed down, enraptured, at the newborn, who waved his arms and kicked his little legs in the delight of being free at last from his long confinement.

"Oh, Larry, he's beautiful," breathed Angela, in the manner of new mothers everywhere. Already the pangs of childbirth and the long and agonizing travail of labor were forgotten. The only reality was the baby in her arms and the future they would have together.

"He sure is," a smiling Larry agreed. "Smart, too. Look at that face. Hi, little guy," and he touched one gentle finger to the infant's soft cheek.

"Little angel, I'm your momma, yes . . . ," cooed Angela.

"And I'm your—" But *what* was he? Larry looked at Angela with a question mark openly in his eyes. He was remembering all the many good times they'd had together in their marriage, when their love was new. He was remembering how close they had been, how affectionate. Angela returned the same look, tentative, hoping, almost fearing . . .

"Angela? Could we give it another chance?" Larry held his breath.

She smiled almost shyly. "I'd like that, Larry," answered Angela in a low, soft voice. She raised her face to his, and he kissed her gently. They both gazed down worshipfully at the baby.

"I'm your dad," Larry said strongly, proudly. "I'm your dad, and you're my boy."

The three of them cuddled very closely together; they would be close together for always, from this moment on.

And so time passed, as time is wont to do. Alex and Larry got rich, thanks to Expectane, and even more miraculous than their success in business was the success they had in keeping the true story of Alex's experiment a secret from the press and the world. Alex and Diana got married; Larry and Angela got remarried, and both couples bought large, comfortable homes near each other and spent most of their vacations together.

Present-day genetic engineering and biotechnology proclaim that it is possible to impregnate a human male and bring such an infant to term. *Theoretically* possible, that is, because no human—apart from Dr. Alexander Hesse—has yet tried it. In fact, there is a waiting list of males eager to be impregnated, but most of these are transsexuals who want to feel all woman. As for women, they laugh out loud at such a suggestion. Show me the man, they say, who can stand to go through nine months of pregnancy and nine hours of labor, and we'll show you the greatest hero the world has ever produced.

Larry and Angela named their little boy Alexander, but to avoid confusion with the big guy, they call him Zander or Zan. And here's a strange thing. He looks exactly like Larry Arbogast. Maybe, who knows, Angela was off in her timing? Maybe Zander was conceived on the night of the Kellman wedding after all, the night he and Angela had . . . you know.

Anyway, Larry Arbogast thought so, and that was all that mattered.

Junior remains Junior. At the age of one year, she shows all the signs of being the great beauty she will one day be. She is tall, thanks to her swim in Alex's and Diana's gene pool, and strong, and completely sure of herself. She bullies her best friend and constant companion Zander Arbogast unmercifully, and he toddles around after her in a dreamlike trance, completely enthralled. Maybe it's a preview of what their future lives will be.

Today, the babies were playing on the white sand beach together, while their parents basked happily in beach chairs nearby. As usual, Junior had all the toys, while Zan looked on unhappily, whimpering.

"What did we say about sharing, Junior?" chided Diana, ravishing in a one-piece bathing suit that showed off the round bowl of her belly, where Junior's sister or brother was coming along nicely.

"Play nice, you two," added Angela.

The babies babbled joyously at each other.

"Listen to them," said Alex with a smile, stretching his legs out and relaxing in the sun, a totally happy, fulfilled man. "They'll be talking any day now."

"Bet you fifty bucks, my kid says the first word," offered Larry, who was to lose the bet in less than a minute.

The little boy grabbed a toy away from the little girl. Junior turned and looked at the beach chairs and yelled out one word, unmistakably:

"Mama!!"

At the same instant, Alex and Diana leaned forward, and they called back simultaneously, "Yes?!"

They've *got* to stop doing that.